**Praise for the novels of *New York Times*
and *USA TODAY* bestselling author**

DIANA PALMER

"A delightful romance with interesting new characters
and many familiar faces. It's nice to have a hero
who is not picture perfect in looks or instincts,
and a heroine who accepts her privileged life
yet is willing to work for the future she wants."
—*RT Book Reviews* on *Wyoming Tough*

"Palmer demonstrates, yet again, why she's the
queen of desperado quests for justice and true love."
Publishers Weekly on *Dangerous*

"The popular Palmer has penned another winning
novel, a perfect blend of romance and suspense."
—*Booklist* on *Lawman*

"Palmer knows how to make the sparks fly…
heartwarming."
—*Publishers Weekly* on *Renegade*

"Sensual and suspenseful."
—*Booklist* on *Lawless*

"Diana Palmer is a mesmerizing storyteller who
captures the essence of what a romance should be."
—*Affaire de Coeur*

Also available from Diana Palmer and Harlequin HQN

Available Next Month:
INVINCIBLE

Other books by Diana Palmer available in ebook format.

DIANA PALMER

TOUGH TO *Tame*

HARLEQUIN®HQN™

Recycling programs
for this product may
not exist in your area.

ISBN-13: 978-0-373-77942-0

TOUGH TO TAME

Copyright © 2010 by Diana Palmer

This edition published by arrangement with Harlequin Books S.A.

For questions and comments about the quality of this book, please contact us at CustomerService@Harlequin.com.

Printed in U.S.A.

Dear Reader,

Dr. Bentley Rydel turned up in a Harlequin Special Edition I wrote, entitled *Heart of Stone*. He was a veterinarian, crusty and rude, but he had a soft center for animals. I was looking for a minor character to build a book around, and he came to mind.

Well, if he was going to be the hero, I had to have a heroine. So I thought the perfect companion for him would be someone who understood the work. Cappie Drake became one of the veterinary technicians in his practice in Jacobsville, Texas.

Cappie lived with her brother, Kell, who was recovering from injuries he'd sustained working overseas. Her brother was an author, who wrote for various newsmagazines. Their parents died when Cappie was ten. Kell was in the military, so he became responsible for his little sister. They lived all over the world, giving Cappie a sophistication that sat oddly on a young woman in small-town Texas.

They ended up back in Texas when Kell quit the military and devoted himself to reporting. Cappie was working for a veterinarian in San Antonio, and she fell in love with a man who seemed the stuff of dreams. He did have a few rough edges. Once, he grabbed her arm hard to leave a visible bruise. He said it was an accident, and apologized profusely. Kell saw the warning signs and begged her to give him up, but Cappie was in love and she thought her brother was overreacting.

Things didn't improve. The relationship grew more abusive. Finally, Cappie tried to get Frank to admit that he had a drinking problem. He lost his temper and beat her to her knees, breaking her arm in the process. Kell, who was in a wheelchair from an accident overseas on assignment, managed to grab a lamp and knock Frank out before he killed Cappie.

Frank was arrested and sentenced to a jail term for assaulting Cappie. Meanwhile, the Drakes had a cousin in Comanche Wells, Texas, who died and left them a run-down house and a little acreage. Kell insisted that Cappie move down there with him. He knew that Frank would be released in a few months, and that Cappie would need more protection than he could give her. In Jacobsville, near Comanche Wells, he had friends, a few mercenaries with whom he was really working when Cappie thought he was pursuing a career in journalism.

Frank gets out of jail and comes after Cappie. He's found out that she and Dr. Bentley Rydel have a relationship which is heating up by the day. So his first act of revenge is to go to see Bentley and convince him that Cappie is just after his money. Bentley is vulnerable because of an experience in his past with a woman who was pretending to be something she wasn't. He believes Frank, and decides that Cappie must be pushed out of his life. He tells her she's quitting her job so she won't be able to claim unemployment insurance.

Cappie is devastated, but when she gets home she finds her brother, Kell, unconscious and half dead from a beating…and she knows who did it. What she doesn't know is if Kell will live, and if Frank's coming after her….

I had a lot of fun writing about Cappie and Bentley. I love animals, as many of you know, and have lived with a menagerie of dogs, cats, birds, even an emu named George. So having a hero who was a vet, and a heroine who loved animals, too, felt very natural to me.

What also felt natural was setting the book as a Long, Tall Texan. The town, Comanche Wells, is right next to Jacobsville. When I first started writing the series, I had no idea that there would be so many books. The characters needed additional areas in which to live. So Comanche Wells came into being.

This October, there will be another Harlequin Special Edition entitled *Texas Born*. It's a Long, Tall Texan book, and will feature two new characters—Gabriel Brandon and Michelle Godfrey. Sparks fly when these two get together! And readers will get to visit with some of their favorite characters from the series.

But I'm getting ahead of myself—the next book coming your way is in August, *Invincible*, and the story brings two archenemies, Carson and Carlie, together. The two of them find that sometimes preconceived ideas blind people to the real person underneath the mask. And love can heal wounds that have hurt forever, it seems.

And then in November, from Harlequin HQN, we're going back to one of my favorite places, the beautiful state of Wyoming in *Wyoming Strong*. Sara Brandon, Gabriel's sister, moves to a ranch in Wyoming and discovers her next-door neighbor is deliciously handsome, but a man of few words…and she sets out to tame the lone wolf.

There is a lot to read this coming year, and I hope you enjoy the books as much as I loved writing them. Thank you, always, for your friendship and loyalty all these years. You are the reason I keep writing.

Much love, from your biggest fan,

Diana Palmer

I dedicate this book to all the fine veterinarians, technicians, groomers and office workers who do so much every day to keep our furry friends healthy. Thanks!

CHAPTER ONE

CAPPIE DRAKE PEERED around a corner inside the veterinary practice where she worked, her soft gray eyes wide with apprehension. She was looking for the boss, Dr. Bentley Rydel. Just lately, he'd been on the warpath, and she'd been the target for most of the sarcasm and harassment. She was the newest employee in the practice. Her predecessor, Antonia, had resigned and run for the hills last month.

"He's gone to lunch," came an amused whisper from behind her.

Cappie jumped. Her colleague, Keely Welsh Sinclair, was grinning at her. The younger woman, nineteen to Cappie's twenty-three, was only recently married to dishy Boone Sinclair, but she'd kept her job at the veterinary clinic despite her lavish new lifestyle. She loved animals.

So did Cappie. But she'd been wondering if

love of animals was enough to put up with Bentley Rydel.

"I lost the packing slip for the heartworm medicine," Cappie said with a grimace. "I know it's here somewhere, but he was yelling and I got flustered and couldn't find it. He said terrible things to me."

"It's autumn," Keely said.

Cappie frowned. "Excuse me?"

"It's autumn," she repeated.

The older woman was staring blankly at her.

Keely shrugged. "Every autumn, Dr. Rydel gets even more short-tempered than usual and he goes missing for a week. He doesn't leave a telephone number in case of emergencies, he doesn't call here and nobody knows where he is. When he comes back, he never says where he's been."

"He's been like this since I was hired," Cappie pointed out. "And I'm the fifth new vet tech this year, Dr. King said so. Dr. Rydel ran the others off."

"You have to yell back, or just smile when he gets wound up," Keely said in a kindly tone.

Cappie grimaced. "I never yell at anybody."

"This is a good time to learn. In fact…"

"Where the hell is my damned raincoat?!"

Cappie's face was a study in horror. "You said he went to lunch!"

"Obviously he came back," Keely replied, wincing, as the boss stormed into the waiting room where two shocked old ladies were sitting beside cat carriers.

Dr. Bentley Rydel was tall, over six feet, with pale blue eyes that took on the gleam of steel when he was angry. He had jet-black hair, thick and usually untidy because he ran his fingers through it in times of frustration. His feet were large, like his hands. His nose had been broken at some point, which only gave his angular face more character. He wasn't conventionally handsome, but women found him very attractive. He didn't find them attractive. If there was a more notorious woman hater than Bentley Rydel in all of Jacobs County, Texas, it would be hard to find him.

"My raincoat?" he repeated, glaring at Cappie as if it were her fault that he'd left without it.

Cappie drew herself up to her full height—the top of her head barely came to Bentley's shoulder—and took a deep breath. "Sir," she said smartly, "your raincoat is in the closet where you left it."

His dark eyebrows rose half a foot.

Cappie cleared her throat and shook her head as if to clear it. The motion dislodged her precariously placed barrette. Her long, thick blond hair shook free of it, swirling around her shoulders like a curtain of silk.

While she was debating her next, and possibly job-ending, comment, Bentley was staring at her hair. She always wore it on top of her head in that stupid ponytail. He hadn't realized it was so long. His pale eyes narrowed as he studied it.

Keely, fascinated, managed not to stare. She turned to the old ladies watching, spellbound. "Mrs. Ross, if you'll bring—" she looked at her clipboard "—Luvvy the cat on back, we'll see about her shots."

Mrs. Ross, a tiny little woman, smiled and pulled her rolling cat carrier along with her, casting a wistful eye back at the tableau she was reluctantly foregoing.

"Dr. Rydel?" Cappie prompted, because he was really staring.

He scowled suddenly and blinked. "It's raining," he said shortly.

"Sir, that is not my fault," she returned. "I do not control the weather."

"A likely story," he huffed. He turned on his heel, went to the closet, jerked his coat out, displacing everybody else's, and stormed out the door into the pouring rain.

"And I hope you melt!" Cappie muttered under her breath.

"I heard that!" Bentley Rydel called without looking back.

Cappie flushed and moved back behind the counter, trying not to meet Gladys Hawkins's eyes, because the old lady was almost crying, she was laughing so hard.

"There, there," Dr. King, the long-married senior veterinarian, said with a gentle smile. She patted Cappie on the shoulder. "You've done well. By the time she'd been here a month, Antonia was crying in the bathroom at least twice a day, and she never talked back to Dr. Rydel."

"I've never worked in such a place," Cappie said blankly. "I mean, most veterinarians are like you—they're nice and professional, and they don't yell at the staff. And, of course, the staff doesn't yell…"

"Yes, they do," Keely piped in, chuckling. "My husband made the remark that I was a glorified groomer, and the next time he came in here, our groomer gave him an earful about just what a groomer does." She grinned. "Opened his eyes."

"They do a lot more than clip fur," Dr. King agreed. "They're our eyes and ears in between exams. Many times, our groomers have saved lives by noticing some small problem that could have turned fatal."

"Your husband is a dish," Cappie told Keely shyly.

Keely laughed. "Yes, he is, but he's opinionated, hardheaded and temperamental with it."

"He was a tough one to tame, I'll bet," Dr. King mused.

Keely leaned forward. "Not half as tough as Dr. Rydel is going to be."

"Amen. I pity the poor woman who takes him on."

"Trust me, she hasn't been born yet," Keely replied.

"He likes you," Cappie sighed.

"I don't challenge him," Keely said simply. "And I'm younger than most of the staff. He thinks of me as a child."

Cappie's eyes bulged.

Keely patted her on the shoulder. "Some people do." The smile faded. Keely was remembering her mother, who'd been killed by a friend of Keely's father. The whole town had been talking about it. Keely had landed well, though, in Boone Sinclair's strong arms.

"I'm sorry about your mother," Cappie said gently. "We all were."

"Thanks," Keely replied. "We were just getting to know one another when she was…killed. My father plea-bargained himself down to a short jail term, but I don't think he'll be back this way. He's too afraid of Sheriff Hayes."

"Now there's a real dish," Cappie said. "Handsome, brave…"

"…suicidal," Keely interjected.

"Excuse me?"

"He's been shot twice, walking into gun battles," Dr. King explained.

"No guts, no glory," Cappie said.

Her companions chuckled. The phone rang, another customer walked in and the conversation turned to business.

CAPPIE WENT HOME late. It was Friday and the place was packed with clients. Nobody escaped before six-thirty, not even the poor groomer who'd spent half a day on a Siberian husky. The animals had thick undercoats and it was a job to wash and brush them out. Dr. Rydel had been snippier than usual, too, glaring at Cappie as if she were responsible for the overflow of patients.

"Cappie, is that you?" her brother called from the bedroom.

"It's me, Kell," she called back. She put down

her raincoat and purse and walked into the small, sparse bedroom where her older brother lay surrounded by magazines and books and a small laptop computer. He managed a smile for her.

"Bad day?" she asked gently, sitting down beside him on the bed, softly so that she didn't worsen the pain.

He only nodded. His face was taut, the only sign of the pain that ate him alive every hour of the day. A journalist, he'd been on overseas assignment for a magazine when he was caught in a firefight and wounded by shrapnel. It had lodged in his spine where it was too dangerous for even the most advanced surgery. The doctors said someday, the shrapnel might shift into a location where it would be operable. But until then, Kell was basically paralyzed from the waist down. Oddly, the magazine hadn't provided any sort of health care coverage for him, and equally oddly, he'd insisted that he wasn't going to court to force them to pay up. Cappie had wondered at her brother being in such a profession in the first place. He'd been in the army for several years. When he came out, he'd become a journalist. He made an extraordinary living from it. She'd mentioned that to a friend in the newspaper business who'd been astonished.

Most magazines didn't pay that well, he'd noted, eyeing Kell's new Jaguar.

Well, at least they had Kell's savings to keep them going, even if it did so frugally now, after he paid the worst of the medical bills. Her meager salary, although good, barely kept the utilities turned on and food in the aging refrigerator.

"Taken your pain meds?" she added.

He nodded.

"Not helping?"

"Not a lot. Not today, anyway," he added with a forced grin. He was good-looking, with thick short hair even blonder than hers and those pale silvery-gray eyes. He was tall and muscular; or he had been, before he'd been wounded. He was in a wheelchair now.

"Someday they'll be able to operate," she said.

He sighed and managed a smile. "Before I die of old age, maybe."

"Stop that," she chided softly, and bent to kiss his forehead. "You have to have hope."

"I guess."

"Want something to eat?"

He shook his head. "Not hungry."

"I can make southwestern corn soup." It was his favorite.

He gave her a serious look. "I'm impacting your

life. There are places for ex-military where I could stay…"

"No!" she exploded.

He winced. "Sis, it isn't right. You'll never find a man who'll take you on with all this baggage," he began.

"We've had this argument for several months already," she pointed out.

"Yes, since you gave up your job and moved back here with me, after I got…wounded. If our cousin hadn't died and left us this place, we wouldn't even have a roof over our heads, stark as it is. It's killing me, watching you try to cope."

"Don't be melodramatic," she chided. "Kell, all we have is each other," she added somberly. "Don't ask me to throw you out on the street so I can have a social life. I don't even like men much, don't you remember?"

His face hardened. "I remember why, mostly."

She flushed. "Now, Kell," she said. "We promised we wouldn't talk about that anymore."

"He could have killed you," he gritted. "I had to browbeat you just to make you press charges!"

She averted her eyes. Her one boyfriend in her adult life had turned out to be a homicidal maniac when he drank. The first time it happened, Frank Bartlett had grabbed Cappie's arm and left a black bruise. Kell advised her to get away from him, but she, infatuated and rationalizing, said that he hadn't meant it. Kell knew better, but he couldn't convince her. On their fourth date, the boy had taken her to a bar, had a few drinks, and when she gently tried to get him to stop, he'd dragged her outside and lit into her. The other patrons had come to her rescue and one of them had driven her home. The boy had come back, shamefaced and crying, begging for one more chance. Kell had put his foot down and said no, but Cappie was in love and wouldn't listen. They were watching a movie at the rented house, when she asked him about his drinking problem. He'd lost his temper and started hitting her, with hardly any provocation at all. Kell had managed to get into his wheelchair and into the living room. With nothing more than a lamp base as a weapon, he'd knocked the lunatic off Cappie and onto the floor. She was dazed and bleeding, but he'd told her how to tie the boy's thumbs together behind his back, which she'd done while Kell picked up his cell phone and called for law enforcement. Cappie had gone to the hospital and the boy had gone to jail for assault.

With her broken arm in a sling, Cappie had testified against him, with Kell beside her in court as moral support. The sentence, even so, hadn't been extreme. The boy drew six months' jail time and a year's probation. He also swore vengeance. Kell took the threat a great deal more seriously than Cappie had.

The brother and sister had a distant cousin who lived in Comanche Wells, Texas. He'd died a year ago, but the probation of the will had dragged on. Three months ago, Kell had a letter informing her that he and Cappie were inheriting a small house and a postage-stamp-size yard. But it was at least a place to live. Cappie had been uncertain about uprooting them from San Antonio, but Kell had been strangely insistent. He had a friend in nearby Jacobsville who was acquainted with a local veterinarian. Cappie could get a job there, working as a veterinary technician. So she'd given in.

She hadn't forgotten the boy. It had been a wrench, because he was her first real love. Fortunately for her, the relationship hadn't progressed past hot kisses and a little petting, although he'd wanted it to. That had been another sticking point: Cappie's impeccable morals. She was out of touch with the modern world, he'd accused, from living with her overprotective big brother for so long. She needed to loosen up. Easy to say, but Cappie didn't want a casual relationship and she said so. When he drank more than usual, he said it was her fault that he got drunk and hit her, because she kept him so frustrated.

Well, he was entitled to his opinion. Cappie didn't share it. He'd seemed like the nicest, gentlest sort of man when she'd first met him. His sister had brought her dog to the veterinary practice where Cappie worked. He'd been sitting in the truck, letting his sister wrangle a huge German shepherd dog back outside. When he'd seen Cappie, he'd jumped out and helped. His sister had seemed surprised. Cappie didn't notice.

After it was over, Cappie had found that at least two of her acquaintances had been subjected to the same sort of abuse by their own boyfriends. Some had been lucky, like Cappie, and disentangled themselves from the abusers. Others were trapped by fear into relationships they didn't even want. It was hard, she decided, telling by appearance what men would be like when they got you alone. At least Dr. Rydel was obviously violent and dangerous, she told herself. Not that she wanted anything to do with him socially.

"What was that?" Kell asked.

"Oh, I was thinking about one of my bosses," she confided. "Dr. Rydel is a holy terror. I'm scared to death of him."

He scowled. "Surely he isn't like Frank Bartlett?"

"No," she said quickly. "I don't think he'd ever hit a woman. He really isn't the sort. He just blusters and rages and curses. He loves animals. He called the police on a man who brought in a little dog with cuts and bruises all over him. The man had beaten the dog and pretended it had fallen down stairs. Dr. Rydel knew better. He testified against the man and he went to jail."

"Good for Dr. Rydel." He smiled. "If he's that nice to animals, he isn't likely the sort of person who'd hit women," he had to agree. "I was told by my friend that Rydel was a good sort to work for." He frowned. "Your boyfriend kicked your cat on your first date."

She grimaced. "And I made excuses for him." Not long after that, her cat had vanished. She'd often wondered what had happened to him, but he returned after her boyfriend left. "Frank was so handsome, so...eligible," she added quietly. "I guess I was flattered that a man like that would look twice at me. I'm no beauty."

"You are. Inside."

"You're a nice brother. How about that soup?"

He sighed. "I'll eat it if you'll fix it. I'm sorry. About the way I am."

"Like you can help it," she muttered, and smiled. "I'll get it started."

He watched her walk away, thoughtful.

She brought in a tray and had her soup with him. There were just the two of them, all alone in the world. Their parents had died long ago, when she was ten. Kell, who'd been amazingly athletic and healthy in those days, had simply taken over and been a substitute parent to her. He'd been in the military, and they'd traveled all over the world. A good deal of her education had been completed through correspondent courses, although she'd seen a lot of the world. Now, Kell thought he was a burden, but what had she been for all those long years when he'd sacrificed his own social life to raise a heartbroken kid? She owed him a lot. She only wished she could do more for him.

She remembered him in his uniform, an officer, so dignified and commanding. Now, he was largely confined to bed or that wheelchair. It wasn't even a motorized one, because they couldn't afford it. He did continue to work, in his own fashion, at crafting a novel. It was an adventure, based on some knowledge he'd acquired from his military background and a few friends who worked, he said, in covert ops.

"How's the book coming?" she asked.

He laughed. "Actually I think it's going very well. I spoke to a buddy of mine in Washington about some new political strategies and robotic warfare innovations."

"You know everybody."

He made a face at her. "I know almost everybody." He sighed. "I'm afraid the phone bill will be out of sight again this month. Plus I had to order some more books on Africa for the research."

She gave him a look of pride. "I don't care. You accomplish so much," she said softly. "More than a lot of people in much better shape physically."

"I don't sleep as much as most people do," he said wryly. "So I can work longer hours."

"You need to talk to Dr. Coltrain about something to make you sleep."

He sighed. "I did. He gave me a prescription."

"Which you didn't get filled," she accused. "Connie, at the pharmacy, told on you."

"We don't have the money right now," he said gently. "I'll manage."

"It's always money," she said miserably. "I wish I was talented and smart, like you. Maybe I could get a better-paying job."

"You're good at what you do," he replied firmly. "And you love your work. Believe me, that's a lot more important than making a big paycheck. I should know."

She sighed as she sipped her soup. "I guess." She gave him a quick glance. "But it would help with the bills."

"My book is going to make us millions," he told her with a grin. "It will hit the top of the *New York Times* bestseller list, I'll be in demand for talk shows and we'll be able to buy a new car."

"Optimist," she accused.

"Hey, without hope, what have we got?" He looked around with a grimace. "Unpainted walls, cracks in the paint, a car with two hundred thousand miles on it and a leaky roof."

"Oh, darn," she muttered, following his eyes to the yellow spot on the ceiling. "I'll bet another one of those stupid nails worked its way out of the tin. I wish we could have afforded a shingle roof."

"Well, tin is cheaper, and it looks nice."

She looked at him meaningfully.

"It's cheap, anyway," he persisted. "Don't you like the sound of rain on a tin roof? Just listen. It's like music."

It was like a tin drum, she pointed out, but he just laughed.

She smiled. "I guess you're right. It's better not

to wish we had more than we do. We'll get by, Kell," she assured him. "We always do."

"At least we're in it together," he agreed. "But you should think about the military home."

"After I'm dead and buried, you can go into a home," she assured him. "For now, you just eat your soup and hush."

He smiled tenderly. "Okay."

She smiled back. He was the nicest big brother in the whole world, and she wasn't abandoning him while there was a breath in her body.

IT HAD STOPPED raining when she got to work the next morning. She was glad. She hadn't wanted to get out of bed at all. There was something magical about lying in the bed with rain coming down, all safe and cozy and warm. But she wanted to keep her job. She couldn't do both.

She was putting her raincoat in the closet when a long arm presented itself over her shoulder and deposited a bigger raincoat there.

"Hang that up for me, please," Dr. Rydel said gruffly.

"Yes, sir."

She fumbled it onto a hanger. When she closed the door and turned, he was still standing there.

"Is something wrong, sir?" she asked formally.

He was frowning. "No."

But he looked as if he had the weight of the world on his shoulders. She knew how that felt, because she loved her brother and she couldn't help him. Her soft gray eyes looked up into his pale blue ones. "When life gives you lemons, make lemonade?" she ventured.

A laugh escaped his tight control. "What the hell would you know about lemons, at your age?" he asked.

"It isn't the age, Dr. Rydel," she said. "It's the mileage. If I were a car, they'd have to decorate me with solid gold accessories just to get me off the lot."

His eyes softened, just a little. "I suppose I'd be in a junkyard."

She laughed, quickly controlling it. "Sorry."

"Why?"

"You're sort of hard to talk to," she confessed.

He drew in a long breath. Just for a minute, he looked oddly vulnerable. "I'm not used to people. I deal with them in the practice, but I live alone. I have most of my life." He frowned. "Your brother lives with you, doesn't he? Why doesn't he work?"

She tightened up. "He was overseas covering a war and a bomb exploded nearby. He caught shrapnel in the spine and they can't operate. He's paralyzed from the waist down."

He grimaced. "That's a hell of a way to end up in a wheelchair."

"Tell me about it," she agreed quietly. "He was in the military for years, but he got tired of dragging me all over the world, so he mustered out and got a job working for this magazine. He said it would mean he wouldn't be gone so much." She sighed. "I guess he wasn't, but he's in a lot of pain and they can't do much for it." She looked up at him. "It's hard to watch."

For an instant, some fellow feeling flared in his eyes. "Yes. It's easier to hurt yourself than to watch someone you love battle pain." His face softened as he looked down at her. "You take care of him."

She smiled. "Yes. Well, as much as he'll let me, anyway. He took care of me from the age of ten, when our parents died in a wreck. He wants me to let him go into some sort of military home, but I'll never do that."

He looked very thoughtful. And sad. He looked as if he badly needed someone to talk to, but he had nobody. She knew the feeling.

"Life is hard," she said gently.

"Then you die," he added, and managed a smile.

"Back to work, Miss Drake." He hesitated. "Your name, Cappie. What's it short for?"

She hesitated. She bit her lower lip.

"Come on," he coaxed.

She drew in a breath. "Capella," she said.

His eyebrows shot up. "The star?"

She laughed, delighted. Most people had no idea what it meant. "Yes."

"One of your parents was an astronomy buff," he guessed.

"No. My mother was an astronomer, and my father was an astrophysicist," she corrected, beaming. "He worked for NASA for a while."

He pursed his lips. "Brainy people."

"Don't worry, it didn't rub off on me. Kell got all that talent. In fact, he's writing a book, an adventure novel." She smiled. "I just know it's going to be a blockbuster. He'll rake in the money, and then we won't have to worry about money for medicine and health care."

"Health care." He harrumphed. "It's a joke. People going without food to buy pills, without clothes to afford gas, having to choose between essentials and no help anywhere to change things."

She was surprised at his attitude. Most people seemed to think that health care was available to everybody. Actually she could only afford basic

coverage for herself. If she ever had a major medical emergency, she'd have to beg for help from
the state. She hoped she could even get it. It still
amazed her that Kell's employers hadn't offered
him health care benefits. "We don't live in a perfect society," she agreed.

"No. Nowhere near it."

She wanted to ask him why he was so outspo-
ken on the issue, which hit home for her, too. But
before she could overcome her shyness, the phones
were suddenly ringing off the hook and three new
four-legged patients walked in the door with their
owners. One of them, a big Boxer, made a beeline
for a small poodle whose owner had let it come in
without a lead.

"Grab him!" Cappie called, diving after the
Boxer.

Dr. Rydel followed her, gripping the Boxer's
lead firmly. He pulled up on it just enough to es-
tablish control, and held it so that the dog's head
was erect. "Down, sir!" he said in a commanding
tone. "Sit!"

The Boxer sat down at once. So did all the pet
owners. Cappie burst out laughing. Dr. Rydel gave
her a speaking glance, turned, and led the Boxer
back to the patient rooms without a single word.

CHAPTER TWO

WHEN SHE GOT home, Cappie told her brother about the struggle with the Boxer, and its result. He roared with laughter. It had been a long time since she'd seen him laugh.

"Well, at least he can control animals and people," he told her.

"Indeed he can." She picked up the dirty dishes and stacked them from their light supper. "You know, he's very adamant about health care. For people, I mean. I wonder if he has somebody who can't afford medicines or doctors or hospitals? He never talks about his private life."

"Neither do you," he pointed out dryly.

She made a face. "I'm not interesting. Nobody would want to know what I do at home. I just cook and clean and wash dishes. What's exciting about that? When you were in the army, you knew movie stars and sports legends."

"They're just like you and me," he told her. "Fame isn't a character reference. Neither is wealth."

"Well, I wouldn't mind being rich," she sighed. "We could fix the roof."

"One day," he promised her, "we'll get out of the hole."

"You think?"

"Miracles happen every day."

She wasn't touching that line with a pole. Just lately, she'd have given blood for a miracle that would treat her just to a new raincoat. The one she had, purchased for a dollar at a thrift shop, was worn and faded and missing buttons. She'd sewed others on, but none of them matched. It would be so nice to have one that came from a store, brand-new, with that smell that clothes had when nobody had ever worn them before.

"What are you thinking about?" Kell asked.

"New raincoats," she sighed. Then she saw his expression and grimaced. "Sorry. Just a stray thought. Don't mind me."

"Santa Claus might bring you one," he said.

She glowered at him on her way out the door. "Listen, Santa Claus couldn't find this place if he had GPS on his sleigh. And if he did, his reindeer would slide off the tin roof and fall to their doom, and we'd get sued."

He was still laughing when she got to the kitchen.

IT WAS GETTING close to Christmas. Cappie dug out the old, faded artificial Christmas tree and put it up in the living room where Kell could see it from his hospital bed. She had one new string of mini-lights, all she could afford, and she put the old ornaments on it. Finally she plugged in the tree. It became a work of art, a magical thing, when she turned out the other lights and looked at it.

"Wow," Kell said in a soft tone.

She moved to the doorway and smiled at him. "Yeah. Wow." She sighed. "Well, at least it's a tree. I wish we could have a real one."

"Me, too, but you spent every Christmas sick in bed until we realized you were allergic to fir trees."

"Bummer."

He burst out laughing. "Now, all we have to do is decide what we're going to put under it."

"Artificial presents, I guess," she said quietly.

"Stop that. We're not destitute."

"Yet."

"What am I going to do with you? There is a

Santa Claus, 'Virginia,'" he chided. "You just don't know it yet."

She turned the lights back on and smiled at him. "Okay. Have it your way."

"And we'll put presents under it."

Only if they come prepaid and already wrapped, she thought cynically, but she didn't say it. Life was hard, when you lived on the fringes of society. Kell had a much better attitude than she did. Her optimism was losing ground by the day.

THE BEGINNING OF the week started out badly. Dr. Rydel and Dr. King had a very loud and disturbing argument over possible treatments for a beautiful black Persian male cat with advanced kidney failure.

"We can do dialysis," Dr. King argued.

Dr. Rydel's pale blue eyes threw off sparks. "Do you intend to contribute to the 'let's prolong Harry's suffering' fund?"

"Excuse me?"

"His owner is retired. All she has is her social security, because her pension plan crashed and burned during the economic downturn," he said hotly. "How the hell do you think she's going to afford dialysis for a cat who's got, at the most, a couple of weeks of acute suffering to go before he faces an end to the pain?"

Dr. King was giving him very odd looks. She didn't say anything.

"I can irrigate him and pump drugs into him and keep him alive for another month," he said through his teeth. "And he'll be in agony all that time. I can do dialysis and prolong it even more. Or do you think that animals don't really feel pain at all?"

She still hadn't spoken. She just looked at him.

"Dialysis!" he scoffed. "I love animals, too, Dr. King, and I'd never give up on one that had a ghost of a chance of a normal life. But this cat isn't having a normal life— he's going through hell on a daily basis. Or haven't you ever seen a human being in the final stages of kidney failure?" he demanded.

"No, I haven't," Dr. King said, in an unusually gentle tone.

"You can take it from me that it's the closest thing to hell on earth. And I am not, repeat not, putting the cat on dialysis and that's the advice I'm giving his owner."

"Okay."

He frowned. "Okay?"

She didn't smile. "It must have been very hard to watch," she added quietly.

His face, for an instant, betrayed the anguish of a personal loss of some magnitude. He turned away and went back into his office. He didn't even slam the door.

Cappie and Keely flanked Dr. King, all big eyes and unspoken questions.

"You don't know, do you?" she asked. She motioned them off into the chart room and closed the door. "You didn't hear me say this," she instructed, and waited until they both nodded. "His mother was sixty when they diagnosed her with kidney failure three years ago. They put her on dialysis and gave her medications to help put off the inevitable, but she lost the battle just a year later when they discovered an inoperable tumor in her bladder. She was in agony. All that time, she had only her social security and Medicaid to help. Her husband, Dr. Rydel's stepfather, wouldn't let him help at all. In fact, Dr. Rydel had to fight just to see his mother. He and his stepfather have been enemies for years, and it just got worse when his mother was so ill. His mother died and he blames his stepfather, first for not letting her go to a doctor for tests in the first place, and then for not letting him help with the costs afterward. She lived in terrible poverty. Her husband was too proud to accept a dime from any other source, and he worked as a night watchman in a manufacturing company."

No wonder Dr. Rydel was so adamant about health care, Cappie thought. She saw him through different eyes. She also understood his frustration.

"He's right, too, about Harry's owner," Dr. King added. "Mrs. Trammel doesn't have much left after she pays her own medicine bills and utilities and groceries. Certainly she doesn't have enough to afford expensive treatments for an elderly cat who doesn't have long to live no matter what we do." She grimaced. "It's wonderful that we have all these new treatments for our pets. But it's not good that we sometimes make decisions that aren't realistic. The cat is elderly and in constant pain. Are we doing it a favor to order thousands of dollars of treatments that its owner can't afford, just to prolong the suffering?"

Keely shrugged. "Bailey, Boone's German shepherd, would have died if Dr. Rydel hadn't operated on him when he got bloat," she ventured.

"Yes, and he's old, too," Dr. King agreed. "But Boone could afford it."

"Good point," Keely agreed.

"We do have medical insurance for pets now," Cappie pointed out.

"It's the same moral question, though," Dr. King pointed out. "Should we do something just because we can do it?"

The phone rang, both lines at once, and a woman with a cat in a blanket and red, tear-filled eyes rushed in the door calling for help.

"It's going to be a long day," Dr. King sighed.

CAPPIE TOLD HER brother about Dr. Rydel's mother. "I guess we're not the only people who wish we had adequate health care," she said, smiling gently.

"I guess not. Poor guy." He frowned. "How do you make a decision like that for a pet?" he added.

"We didn't. We recommend what we thought best, but let Mrs. Trammel make the final decision. She was more philosophical than all of us put together. She said Harry had lived for nineteen good years, been spoiled rotten and shame on us for thinking death was a bitter end. She thinks cats go to a better place, too, and that they have green fields to run through and no cars to run over them." She smiled. "In the end, she decided that it was kinder to just let Dr. Rydel do what was necessary. Keely's barn cat has a new litter of kittens, solid white with blue eyes. She promised Mrs. Trammel one. Life goes on."

"Yes." He was somber. "It does."

She lifted her eyebrows. "Any day now, there's going to be a breakthrough in medical research and you're going to have an operation that will put you back on your feet and give you a new lease on life."

"After which I'll win the British Open, effect détente with the eastern communists and perfect a cure for cancer," he added dryly.

"One miracle at a time," she interrupted. "And just how would you win the British Open? You don't even play tennis!"

"Don't confuse me with a bunch of irrelevant facts." He sank back into his pillows and grimaced. "Besides, the pain is going to kill me long before they find any miraculous surgical techniques." He closed his eyes with a long sigh. "One day without pain," he said quietly. "Just one day. I'd do almost anything for it."

She knew, as many other people didn't, that chronic pain brought on a kind of depression that was pervasive and dangerous. Even the drugs he took for pain only took the edge off. Nothing they'd ever given him had stopped it.

"What you need is a nice chocolate milkshake and some evil, fattening, over-salted French fries and a cholesterol-dripping hamburger," she said.

He made a tortured face. "Go ahead, torment me!"

She grinned. "I overpaid the hardware bill and got sent a ten dollar refund," she said, reaching into her purse. "I'll go to the bank, cash it and we'll eat out tonight!"

"You beauty!" he exclaimed.

She curtsied. "I'll be back before you know it." She glanced at her watch. "Oops, better hurry or the bank will be closed!"

She grabbed her old denim jacket and her purse and ran out the door.

The ancient car was temperamental. It had over two hundred thousand miles on it, and it looked like a piece of junk. She coaxed it into life and grimaced as she read the gas gauge. She had a fourth of a tank left. Well, it was only a five-minute drive to Jacobsville from Comanche Wells. She'd have enough to get her to work and back for one more day. Then she'd worry about gas. The ten-dollar check would have come in handy for that, but Kell needed cheering up more. These spells of depression were very bad for him, and they were becoming more frequent. She'd have done anything to keep him optimistic. Even walking to work.

She cashed the check with two minutes to spare before the bank closed. Then she drove to the local fast-food joint and ordered burgers and fries and milkshakes. She paid for them—had five cents left over—and pulled out into the road. Then two things went wrong at once. The engine quit and a car flew out of a side road and right into the passenger side of her car.

She sat, shaking, amid the ruins of her car, with chocolate milkshake all over her jeans and jacket, and pieces of hamburgers on the dirty floorboard. It was quite an impact. She couldn't move for a minute. She sat, staring at the dash, wondering how she'd manage without a car, because her insurance only covered liability. She had nothing that would even pay to repair the car, if it could be repaired.

She turned her head in slow motion and looked at the car that had hit her. The driver got out, staggering. He laughed. That explained why he'd shot through a stop sign without braking. He leaned against his ruined fender and laughed some more.

Cappie wondered if he had insurance. She also wondered if she didn't have a tire iron that she could get to, before the police came to save the man.

Her car door was jerked open. She looked up into a pair of steely ice-blue eyes.

"Are you all right?" he asked.

She blinked. Dr. Rydel. She wondered where he'd come from.

"Cappie, are you all right?" he repeated. His voice was very soft, nothing like the glitter in those pale eyes.

"I think so," she said. Time seemed to have slowed to a stop. She couldn't get her sluggish brain to work. "I was taking hamburgers and shakes home to Kell," she said. "He was so depressed. I thought it would cheer him up. I was worried about spending the money on treats instead of gas." She laughed dully. "I guess I won't need to worry about gas, now," she added, looking around at the damage.

"You're lucky you weren't in one of the newer little cars. You'd be dead."

She looked toward the other driver. "Dr. Rydel, do you have a tire tool I could borrow?" she asked conversationally.

He saw where she was looking. "You don't want to upset the police, Cappie."

"I won't tell if you won't."

Before he could reply, a Jacobsville police car roared up, lights flashing, and stopped. Obviously somebody in the fast-food place had called them.

Officer Kilraven climbed out of the police car and headed right for Cappie.

"Oh, good, it's him," Cappie said. "He'll scare the other driver to death."

Kilraven bent down on Cappie's side of the car. "You okay? Need an ambulance?"

"Heavens, no," she said quickly. As if she could afford to pay for that! "I'm fine. Just shaken up." She nodded toward the giggling driver who'd hit her. "Dr. Rydel won't loan me a tire iron, so could you shoot that man in the foot for me, please? I don't even have collision insurance and it wasn't my fault. I'll be walking to work on account of him."

"I can't shoot him," Kilraven said with a twinkle in his silver eyes. "But if he tries to hit me, I'll take him to detention in the trunk of my car. Okay?"

She brightened. "Okay!"

He straightened and said something to Dr. Rydel. A minute later, he marched over to the drunk man, smelled his breath, made a face and asked him to perform a sobriety test, which the subject refused. That would mean a blood test at the hospital, which Kilraven was fairly certain the man would fail. He told him he was under arrest and cuffed him. Cappie vaguely heard him calling for a wrecker and backup.

"A wrecker?" She groaned. "I can't afford a wrecker."

"Just don't worry about it right now. Come on. I'll drive you home."

He helped her out of the car. She retrieved her purse, wincing. "I hope he has a Texas-size hangover when he wakes up tomorrow," she said coldly, watching Kilraven putting the prisoner in the back of his squad car. The man was still laughing.

"Oh, I hope he gets pregnant," Dr. Rydel mused, "and it's twins."

She laughed huskily. "Even better. Thanks."

He put her into his big Land Rover. "Wait here. I'll just be a minute."

She sat quietly, fascinated with the interior of the vehicle. It conjured up visions of the African veldt, of elephants and giraffes and wildebeest. She wished she could afford even a twenty-year-old version of this beast. She'd never have to worry about bad roads again.

He was back shortly with a bag and a cup carrier. He put them in her lap. "Two hamburgers and fries and two chocolate shakes."

"How...?"

"Well, it's easier to tell when you're wearing parts of them," he pointed out, indicating chocolate milk stains and mustard and catsup and pieces of food all over her clothes. "Fasten your seat belt."

She did. "I'll pay you back," she said firmly.

He grinned. "Whatever."

He started the engine and drove her out of town. "You'll have to direct me. I don't know where you live."

She named the road, and then the street. They didn't talk. He pulled up in the front yard of the dinky little house, with its peeling paint and rickety steps and sagging eaves.

He grimaced.

"Hey, don't knock it," she said. "It's got a pretty good roof and big rooms and it's paid for. A distant cousin willed it to us."

"Nice of him. Do you have any other cousins?"

"No. It's just me and Kell."

"No other siblings?"

She shook her head. "We don't have any family left."

He gave the house a speaking look.

"If we had the money to fix it up, it would look terrific," she said.

He helped her out of the car and onto the porch. He hesitated about handing her the bag with the food and the carrier of milkshakes.

"Would you like to come in and meet Kell?" she ventured. "Only if you want to," she added quickly.

"Yes, I would."

She unlocked the door and motioned him in. "Kell, I'm home!" she called. "I brought company."

"If it's wearing lipstick and has a good sense of humor, bring it in here quick!" he quipped.

Dr. Rydel burst out laughing. "Sorry, I don't wear lipstick," he called back.

"Oops."

Cappie laughed and walked toward the room a little unsteadily, motioning the vet to follow her.

Kell was propped up in bed with the old laptop. He paused, eyebrows arched, as they walked in. "We should have ordered more food," he said with a grin.

Cappie winced. "Well, see, the food is the problem. I was pulling out of the parking lot and the engine died. A drunk man ran into the car and pretty much killed it."

"Luckily he didn't kill you," Kell said, frowning. "Are you all right?"

"Just bruised a little. Dr. Rydel was kind enough to bring me home. Dr. Rydel, this is my brother, Kell," she began.

"You're the veterinarian?" Kell asked, and his silvery-gray eyes twinkled. "I thought you had fangs and a pointed tail…"

"Kell!" she burst out, horrified.

Dr. Rydel chuckled. "Only during office hours," he returned.

"I'll kill you!" she told her brother.

"Now, now," Dr. Rydel said complacently. "We all know I'm a horror to work for. He's just saying what you aren't comfortable telling me."

"And he does have a sense of humor," Kell said. "Thanks for bringing her home," he added, and the smile faded. "My driving days are apparently over."

"There are vehicles with hand controls now," Dr. Rydel pointed out.

"We're ordering one of those as soon as we get our new yacht paid off," Kell replied with a serious expression.

Cappie burst out laughing. "And our dandy indoor swimming pool."

Dr. Rydel smiled. "At least you still have a sense of humor."

"It's the only part of me that works," Kell replied. "I've offered to check myself into a military home, but she won't hear of it."

"Over my dead body," she reiterated, and glared at him.

He sighed. "It's nice to be loved, but you can take family feeling over the cliff with you, darlin'," he reminded her.

"Sink or swim, we're a matched set," she said stubbornly. "I'm not putting you out on the street."

"Military homes can be very nice," Kell began.

Cappie grimaced. "Your milkshake is getting warm," she interrupted. She took the carrier from Dr. Rydel and handed one to Kell, along with a straw. "There's your burger and fries," she said. "Working?"

"Taking a short break to play mah-jongg," he replied. "I'm actually winning, too."

"I play Sudoku," Dr. Rydel commented.

Kell groaned. "I can't do numbers. I tried that game and thought I'd go nuts. I couldn't even get one column to line up. How do you do it?"

"I'm left-brained," the other man said simply. "Numbers and science. I'd have loved to be a writer, but I'm spelling-challenged."

Kell laughed. "I'm left-brained, too, but I can't handle Sudoku. I can spell, however," he added, tongue in cheek.

"That's why we have a bookkeeper," Dr. Rydel said. "I think people would have issues if their names and animal conditions were constantly misspelled. I had a time in college."

"So did I," Kell confessed. "College trigonometry almost kept me from getting my degree in the first place. I also had a bad time with biology," he added pointedly.

Dr. Rydel grinned. "My best subject. All A's."

"I'll bet the biology-challenged loved you," Cappie said with a chuckle. "Blew the curve every time, didn't you?"

He nodded. "I bought pizzas for my classmates every Saturday night to make it up to them."

"Pizza," Cappie mused. "I remember what that tastes like. I think."

"I don't want to talk about pizza," Kell said and sipped his milkshake. "You and your mushrooms!"

"He hates mushrooms, and I hate Italian sausage," Cappie commented. "I love mushrooms."

"Yuuuuck," Kell commented.

She smiled. "We'll leave you to your supper. If you need anything, call me, okay?"

"Sure. What would you like to be called?"

She wrinkled her nose at him and went out the door.

"Nice to have met you," Kell told the vet.

"Same here," Dr. Rydel said.

He followed Cappie out into the living room. "You'd better eat your own burger and fries before they're cold," he said. "They don't reheat well."

She smiled shyly. "Thanks again for bringing me home, and for the food." She wondered how she was going to get to work the following Monday, but she knew she'd come up with something. She could always beg one of the other vet techs for a ride.

"You're welcome." He stared down at her quietly, frowning. "You sure you're all right?"

She nodded. "I'm wobbly. That's because I was scared to death. I'll be fine. It's just a little bruising. Honest."

"Would you tell me if it was more?" he asked.

She grinned.

"Well, if you think you need to go to the doctor later, you call me. Call the office," he added. "They'll take a message and page me, wherever I am."

"That's very nice of you. Thanks."

He drew in a long breath. His blue eyes narrowed on her face. "You've got a lot on your shoulders for a woman your age," he said quietly.

"Some people have a lot more," she replied. "I love my brother."

He smiled. "I noticed that."

She studied him curiously. "Do you have family?"

His face tautened. "Not anymore."

"I'm sorry."

"People get old. They die." He became distant. "We'll talk another time. Good evening."

"Good evening. Thanks."

He shrugged. "No problem."

She watched him go with a strange sense of loss. He was in many ways the saddest person she'd ever known.

She finished her supper and went to collect her brother's food containers.

"Your boss is nice," he said. "Not what I expected."

"How could you tell him what I said about him, you horrible man?" she asked with mock anger.

"He's one of those rare souls who never lie," he said simply. "He comes at you head-on, not from ambush."

"How do you know that?"

"It's in his manner," he said simply. He smiled. "I'm that way myself. It does take one to know one. Now come here and sit down and tell me what happened."

She drew in a deep breath and sat down in the chair beside the bed. She hated having to tell him the whole truth. It wasn't going to be pretty.

CHAPTER THREE

CAPPIE HITCHED A ride to work with Keely, promising not to make a regular thing of it.

"I'll just have to get another car," she said, as if all that required was a trip to a car lot. In fact, she had no idea what she was going to do.

"My brother is best friends with Sheriff Hayes Carson," Keely reminded her, "and Hayes knows Kilraven. He told him the particulars, and Kilraven had a talk with the driver's insurance company." She chuckled. "I understand some interesting what-if's were mentioned. The upshot is that the driver's insurance is going to pay to fix your car."

"What?"

"Well, he was drunk, Cappie. In fact, he's occupying a cell at the county detention center as we speak. You could sue his insurance company for enough to buy a new Jaguar like my brother's got."

She didn't mention that Kell had owned a Jaguar, and not too long ago. Those days seemed very far away now. "Wow. I've never sued anybody, you know."

Keely laughed. "Me, neither. But you could. Once the insurance people were reminded of that, they didn't seem to think fixing an old car was an extravagant use of funds."

"It's really nice of them," Cappie said, stunned. It was like a miracle. "I didn't know what I was going to do. My brother is an invalid, and the only money we've got is his savings and what I bring home. That's not a whole lot."

"Before I married Boone, I had to count pennies," the other girl said. "I know what it's like to have very little. I think you do very well."

"Thanks." She sighed. "You know, Kell was in the military for years and years. He went into all sorts of dangerous situations, but he never got hurt. Then he left the army and went to work for this magazine, went to Africa to cover a story and got hit with shrapnel from an exploding shell. Go figure."

Keely frowned. "Didn't he have insurance? Most magazines have it for their employees, I'm sure."

"Well, no, he didn't. Odd, isn't it?"

"They sent him to Africa to do a story," Keely added. "What sort of story? A news story?"

Cappie blinked. "You know, I never asked him. I only knew he was leaving the country. Then I got a call from him, saying he was in the hospital with some injuries and he'd be home when he could get here. He wouldn't even let me visit him. An ambulance brought him to our rented house in San Antonio."

Keely didn't say what she was thinking. But she almost had to bite her tongue.

Cappie stared at her. "That's a very strange story, even if I'm the one telling it," she said slowly.

"Maybe it's the truth," Keely said comfortingly. "After all, it's very often stranger than fiction."

"I guess so." She let it drop. But she did intend to talk it over with Kell that night.

WHEN SHE GOT home, there was a big SUV parked in the driveway. She frowned at it as she went up the steps and into the house. The door was unlocked.

She heard laughter coming from Kell's room.

"I'm home!" she called.

"Come on in here," Kell called back. "I've got company."

She took off her coat and moved into the bedroom. Kell's visitor was very tall and lean, with faint silvering at the temples of his black hair. He had green eyes and a somber face, and one of his hands seemed to be burned. He moved it unobtrusively into his pocket when he saw her eyes drawn to it.

"This is an old friend of mine," Kell said. "My sister, Cappie. This is Cy Parks. He owns a ranch in Jacobsville."

Cappie held out her hand, smiling, and shook the one offered. "Nice to meet you."

"Same here. You'll have to bring Kell over to the ranch to see us," he added. "I have a terrific wife and two little boys. I'd love for you to meet them."

"You, with a wife and kids," Kell said, shaking his head. "I'd never have imagined it in my wildest dreams."

"Oh, it comes to all of us, sooner or later," Cy replied lazily. He pursed his lips. "So you work for Bentley Rydel, do you?"

She nodded.

"Does he really carry a pitchfork, or is that just malicious gossip?" Cy added, tongue in cheek.

She flushed. "Kell…!" she muttered at her brother.

He held up both hands and laughed. "I didn't tell him what you said. Honest."

"He didn't," Cy agreed. "Actually Bentley makes a lot of calls at my place during calving season. He's our vet. Good man."

"Yes, he is," Cappie said. "He brought me home after a drunk ran into my car."

Cy's expression darkened. "I heard about that. Tough break."

"Well, the man's insurance company is going to fix our car," Cappie added with a laugh. "It seems they were worried that we might sue."

"We would have," Kell said, and he wasn't smiling. "You could have been killed."

"I just got bruised a little," she said, smiling. "Nice of you to worry, though."

Kell grinned. "It's a hobby of mine."

"You need to get out more," Cy told the man in the bed. "I know you've got pain issues, but staying cooped up in here is just going to make things worse. Believe me, I know."

Kell's eyes darkened. "I guess you're right. But I do have something to do. I'm working on a novel. One about Africa."

Cy Parks's face grew hard. "That place has made its mark on several of us," he said enigmatically.

"It's still making marks on other men," Kell said.

"The Latin American drug cartels are moving in there, as well," Cy replied. "Hell of a thing, as if Africa didn't have enough internal problems as it is."

"As long as power-hungry tyrants can amass fortunes by oppressing other men, it won't lower the casualty rates for any combatants working there," Kell muttered.

"Combatants?" Cappie asked curiously.

"Two groups of people are fighting for supremacy," Kell told her.

"One good, one evil," she guessed.

"No. As far as African internal politics go, both sides have positive arguments. The outsiders are the ones causing the big problems. Their type of diplomacy is most often practiced with rapid-firing automatic weapons and various incendiary devices."

"And IEDs," Cy added.

Cappie blinked. "Excuse me?"

"Improvised explosive devices," Kell translated.

"Were you in the military, too, Mr. Parks?" Cappie asked.

Cy hesitated. "Sort of. Look at the time," he remarked, glancing at his watch. "Lisa wants me to go with her to pick out a new playpen for our youngest son," he added with a grin. "Our toddler more or less trashed the first one."

"Strong kid," Kell noted.

"Yes. Bullheaded, too."

"I wonder where he gets that from," Kell wondered aloud, with twinkling eyes.

"I am not bullheaded," Cy said complacently. "I simply have a resistance to stupid ideas."

"Same difference."

Cy made a face. "I'll come back and check on you later in the week. If you need anything…"

Kell smiled. "Thanks, Cy."

"I'd have come with Eb and Micah when they dropped by," Cy added, "but we were out of town with the kids. It's good to see you again."

"Same here," Kell said. "I owe you."

"For what?" Cy shrugged. "Friends help friends."

"They do."

Cappie stared at her brother with a blank expression. A whole conversation seemed to be going on under her nose that she didn't comprehend.

"I'll see you," Cy said. "Nice to have met you, Miss Drake," he added, smiling.

"You, too," she replied.

Cy left without a backward glance.

After he drove away, Cappie was still staring at her brother. "You didn't say you had friends here. Why haven't I seen them?"

"They came while you were at work," he said. "Several times."

"Oh."

He averted his eyes. "I met them when I was in

the service," he said. "They're fine men. A little unorthodox, but good people."

"Oh!" She relaxed. "Mr. Parks has an injury."

"Yes. He was badly burned trying to save his wife and child from a fire. He was the only one who got out. It turned him mean. But now he's remarried and has two sons, and he seems to have put the past behind him."

"Poor guy." She grimaced. "No wonder he was mean. Who were the other men he mentioned?"

"Other friends. Eb Scott and Micah Steele. Micah's a doctor in Jacobsville. Eb Scott has a sort of training center for paramilitary units."

She blinked. "You do seem to attract the oddest friends."

"Men with guns." He nodded. He grinned.

She laughed. "Okay. I'm stonewalled. What do you want for supper?"

"Nothing heavy," he said. "I had a big lunch."

"You did?" She didn't recall leaving anything out for him except sandwiches in a Baggie.

"Cy brought a whole menu full of stuff from the local Chinese restaurant," he said. "The remains are in the fridge. I wouldn't mind having some of them for supper."

"Chinese food? Real Chinese food, from a real restaurant, that I don't have to cook?" She felt her forehead. "Maybe I'm delusional."

He chuckled. "It does sound like that, doesn't it? Go dig in. Bring me some of the pork and noodles, if you will. There's sticky rice and mangoes for dessert, too."

"I have died and am now in heaven," she said in a haunted tone.

"Me, too. Get cracking. I'm on the fourth chapter of this book already!"

"You are?" She laughed. He looked so much more cheerful. More than he'd been in weeks. "Okay, then."

He pulled the laptop back into place.

"Do I get to read it?"

He nodded. "When it's done."

"That's a deal." She went into the kitchen and got out the boxes of Chinese food. It was all she could do to keep back the tears. Cy Parks was a nice man. A very nice man. Except for their splurged hamburgers and milkshakes, for which she still owed Dr. Rydel she reminded herself, there hadn't been any convenience food for a long time. This was a feast. She put some of it in the freezer for hard times and heated up the rest. Her day was already getting better.

It GOT EVEN better than that. A tall man with sandy hair and blue eyes came driving up in Cappie's own car two days later. The big SUV was following close behind. Cappie gaped at the sight. Her old car had been refurbished, its dents beaten out and the whole thing repainted and repaired. There were even seat covers and floor mats. She stared at it helplessly surprised.

Cy Parks got out of the SUV and followed the sandy-haired man up onto the porch. "I hope you like blue," he told Cappie. "There was a paint sale."

She could barely manage words. "Mr. Parks, I don't even know what to say…" She burst into tears. "It's so kind!"

He patted her awkwardly on the shoulder. "There, there, it's just one of those random acts of kindness we're supposed to pass around. You can do the same thing for somebody else one day."

She dabbed at her eyes. "When I strike it rich, I swear I will!"

He chuckled. "Harley Fowler, here," he introduced his companion, "is as good a mechanic as he is a ranch foreman. I had him supervise the work on your car. The insurance company paid for it all," he added when she started to protest. He grinned. "We get things done here in Jacobsville. The insurance agent locally is the sister-in-law of my top wrangler."

"Well, thank you both," she said huskily. "Thank you so much. I was almost ashamed to ask Keely for rides. She's so nice, but it was an imposition. I live five miles out of her way."

"You're very welcome."

The front door opened and Kell wheeled himself out onto the porch. He whistled when he saw the car. "Good grief, that was quick work," he said.

Cy grinned. "You might remember that I always did know how to cut through the red tape."

"Thanks," Kell told him. "From both of us. If I can ever do anything for you…"

"You've done enough," Cy returned quietly. His green eyes twinkled. "But you could always put me in that novel you're writing. I'd like to be twenty-seven, drop-dead handsome and a linguist."

Kell rolled his eyes. "You can barely speak English," he pointed out.

Cy glared at him. "You take that back, or I'll have Harley shoot all the tires out on this car."

Kell held up both hands, his silver eyes twinkling. "Okay, you could get work as a translator at the UN any day. Honest."

Cy sighed. "Don't I wish." He frowned. "Do you still speak Farsi?"

Kell nodded, smiling.

"I've got a friend who's applying for a job with the company. Think you could tutor him? He's well-off, and he'd pay you for your time."

Kell frowned.

"It's not charity," Cy muttered, glowering at him. "This is a legitimate need. The guy wants to work overseas, but he'll never get the job unless he can perfect his accent."

Kell relaxed. "All right, then. I'll take him on. And thanks."

Cy smiled. "Thank you," he replied. "He's a nice guy. You'll like him." He glanced at Cappie, who was wondering what sort of company Cy's friend worked for. "You won't," he assured her. "I used to be a woman hater, but this guy makes me look civilized. He'll need to come over when you're at work."

Cappie was curious. "Why does he hate women?"

"I think he was married to one," Cy mused.

"Well, that certainly explains that," Kell chuckled.

"Thank you very much for fixing up my car," Cappie told Cy. "I won't forget it."

"No problem. We were glad to help. Oh, mustn't forget the keys, Harley!"

Harley handed the keys to her as Cy headed back and got into the other vehicle. "She purrs like a kitten now," Harley told her. "She drives good."

"The car is a girl?" she asked.

"Only when a guy is driving it," Kell told her with a wicked grin.

"Amen," Harley told him.

"Come on, Harley," Cy called from the SUV.

"Yes, sir." He grinned at the brother and sister and jumped into the passenger seat in Cy's SUV.

"What a nice man," Cappie said. "Just look, Kell!" She walked out to the car, opened the door and gasped. "They oiled the hinges! It doesn't squeak anymore. And look, they fixed the broken dash and replaced the radio that didn't work..." She started crying again.

"Don't do that," Kell said gently. "You'll have me wailing, too."

She made a face at him. "You have nice friends."

"I do, don't I?" He smiled. "Now you won't have to beg rides."

"It will be a relief, although Keely's been wonderful about it." She glanced at her brother. "I don't think the insurance paid for all this."

"Yes, it did," he said firmly. "Period."

She smiled at him. "Okay. You really do have nice friends."

"You don't know how nice," he told her. "But I may tell you one day. Now let's get back inside. It's cold out here today."

"It is a bit nippy." She turned and followed him inside.

THE WEEK WENT by fast. She got her paycheck on Friday and went shopping early Saturday morning in Jacobsville. Kell had said he'd love a new bathrobe for Christmas, so she went to the department store looking.

It was a surprise when she bumped into Dr. Rydel in the men's department. He gave her a curious look. She didn't realize why until she recalled that she'd left her hair long around her shoulders instead of putting it up. He seemed to find it fascinating.

"Shopping for anything particular?" he asked.

"Yes. Kell wants a bathrobe."

"Christmas shopping," he guessed, and smiled.

"Yes."

"I'm replacing a jacket," he sighed. "I made the mistake of going straight from church on a large animal call. A longhorn bull objected to being used as a pincushion and ripped out the sleeve."

She laughed softly. "Occupational hazard," she said.

He nodded. "Your car looks nice."

"Thanks," she said. She could imagine how her old wreck, even repainted, looked to a man who drove a new Land Rover, but she didn't say so. "Mr. Parks had his foreman supervise the work. The insurance company paid for it."

"Nice of him. He knows your brother?"

"They're friends." She frowned. "Mr. Parks doesn't look like a rancher," she blurted out.

"Excuse me?"

"There's something, I don't know, dangerous about him," she said, searching for the right word. "He's very nice, but I wouldn't want him mad at me."

He grinned. "A few drug dealers in prison could attest to the truth of that statement," he said.

"What?"

"You don't know?"

"Know what?"

"Cy Parks is a retired mercenary," he told her. "He was in some bloody firefights in Africa some years back. More recently, he and two other friends and Harley Fowler shut down a drug distribution center here. There was a gunfight."

"In Jacobsville, Texas?" she exclaimed.

"Yep. Parks is one of the most dangerous men I've ever met. Kind to people he likes. But there aren't many of those."

She felt odd. She wondered how it was that her brother had come to know such a man, because he and Cy seemed to be old friends.

"Where do you go from here?" Dr. Rydel asked suddenly.

She blinked. "I don't know," she blurted out,

flushing. "I mean, I thought I might, well, stop by the game store in the strip mall."

He stared at her blankly. "Game store?"

She cleared her throat. "There's this new video game. 'Halo…'"

"'…ODST,'" he said, with evident surprise. "You're a gamer?"

She cleared her throat again. "Well…yes."

He said something unprintable.

She glared at him. "Dr. Rydel!" she exclaimed. "It's not a vice, you know, playing video games. They release tension and they're fun," she argued.

He chuckled. "I have all three Halo games from Bungie, plus the campaigns," he confessed, naming the famous company whose amazing staff had engineered one of the most exciting video game series of all time. "And the new one that just came out."

Now her jaw fell open. "You do?"

"Yes. I have 'Halo: ODST,'" he said, pursing his lips. "Do you game online?"

She didn't want to confess that she couldn't afford the fees. "I like playing by myself," she said. "Or with Kell. He's crazy about the Halo series."

"So am I," Dr. Rydel told her. His blue eyes twinkled. "Maybe we could play split screen sometime, when we're both free."

She gave him a wicked look. "I can put down

Hunters with a .45 automatic." Hunters were some of the most formidable of the alien Covenant bad guys, fearsome to engage in the Halo game because they were huge and it took a dead shot to hit them in their very few vulnerable places.

He whistled. "Not bad, Miss Drake!"

"Have you been a gamer for a long time?" she asked.

"Since college," he replied, smiling. "You?"

"Since high school. Kell was in the military and a bunch of guys in his unit would come over to the house when they were off duty and play war-game videos. We lived off base." She pursed her lips and her eyes twinkled. "I not only learned how to use tactics and weapons, I also learned a lot of very interesting and useful words to employ when I got killed in the games."

"Bad girl," he chided.

She laughed.

"I'll probably see you in the video store," he added.

She beamed. "You probably will."

He grinned and went back to the suits.

FIFTEEN MINUTES LATER, she parked in front of the video store and went inside. It was full of teenage boys mostly, but there were two men standing in front of a rack with the newest sword and sorcery and combat games. One of them was Dr. Rydel. The other, surprisingly, was Officer Kilraven.

Dr. Rydel looked up and smiled when he saw her coming. Kilraven's silver eyes cut around to follow his companion's gaze. His black eyebrows arched.

"She's Christmas shopping," Dr. Rydel announced.

"Buying video games for a relative?" Kilraven wondered aloud.

Dr. Rydel chuckled. "She's a gamer," he confided. "She can take down Hunters with a .45 auto."

Kilraven whistled through his teeth. "Impressive," he said. "I usually do that with a sniper rifle."

"I can use those, too," she said. "But the .45 works just as well, thanks to that magnified sight."

"Have you played all the Halo series?" Kilraven asked.

She nodded. "Now I'm shopping for ODST," she said. "Kell, my brother, likes it, too. He taught me how to play."

Kilraven frowned. "Kell Drake?"

"Yes..."

"I know him," Kilraven replied quietly. "Good man."

"Were you in the army?" she asked innocently.

Kilraven chuckled. "Once, a long time ago."

"Kell only got out a year ago," she said. "He was freelancing for a magazine in Africa and got hit by flying shrapnel. He's paralyzed from the waist down—at least until the shrapnel shifts enough so that they can operate."

Kilraven blinked. "He got hit by flying…he was working for a magazine?" He seemed incredulous. "Doing what?"

"Writing stories."

"Writing stories? Kell can write?"

"He has very good English skills," she began defensively.

"I never," Kilraven said in an odd tone. "Why did he get out of the army?" he wanted to know.

She blinked. "Well, I'm not really sure…" she began.

"Look at this one," Dr. Rydel interrupted helpfully, holding up a game. "Have you ever played this?"

Kilraven was diverted. He took the green case and stared at the description. He grinned. "Have I ever! 'Elder Scrolls IV, Oblivion,'" he murmured. "This is great! You don't have to do the main quest, if you don't want to. There are dozens of other quests. You can even design your own character's appearance, name him, choose from several races…ever played it?" he asked Cappie.

She chuckled. "Actually it's sort of my favorite. I love 'Halo,' but I like using a two-handed sword, as well."

"Vicious girl," Kilraven mused, smiling at her.

Dr. Rydel unobtrusively moved closer to Cappie and cleared his throat. "You shopping or working today?" he asked Kilraven.

The other man looked from Cappie to Dr. Rydel and his silver eyes twinkled. "If you notice, I'm wearing a real uniform," he pointed out. "I even carry a real gun. Now would I be doing that if it was my day off?"

Dr. Rydel smiled back at him. "Would you be shopping for video games on city time?"

Kilraven glared at him. "For your information, I am here detecting crime."

"You are?"

"Absolutely. I have it on good authority that there might be an attempted shoplifting case going on here right now." He raised his voice as he said it and a young boy cleared his throat and eased a game out from under his jacket and back on the shelf. With flaming cheeks he gave Kilraven a hopeful smile and moved quickly to the door.

"If you'll excuse me," Kilraven murmured, "I'm going to have a few helpful words of advice for that young man."

"How did he know?" Cappie asked, stunned, as

she watched the tall officer walk out the door and call to the departing teen.

"Beats me, but I've heard he does things like that." He smiled. "He's on his lunch hour, in case you wondered. I was just ribbing him. I like Kilraven."

She gave him a wry glance. "Sharks like other sharks, do they?" she asked wickedly.

CHAPTER FOUR

AT FIRST, BENTLEY wasn't sure he'd heard her right. Then he saw the demure grin and burst out laughing. She'd compared him to a shark. He was impressed.

"I wondered if you were ever going to learn how to talk to me without getting behind a door first," he mused.

"You're hard going," she confessed. "But so is Kell, to other people. He just walks right over people who don't talk back."

"Exactly," he returned. He shrugged his broad shoulders. "I don't know how to get along with people," he confessed. "My social skills are sparse."

"You're wonderful with animals," she replied.

His eyebrows arched and he smiled. "Thanks."

"Did you always like them?" she wondered.

His eyes had a faraway look. He averted them.

"Yes. But my father didn't. It wasn't until after he died that I indulged my affection for them. It was just my mother and me until I was in high school. That's when she met my stepfather." His expression hardened.

"It must have been very difficult for you," she said quietly, "getting used to another man in your house."

He frowned as he looked down at her. "Yes."

"Oh, I'm remarkably perceptive," she said with amusement in her eyes. "I also suffer from extreme modesty about my other equally remarkable attributes." She grinned.

He laughed again.

Kilraven came back, looking smug.

"You look like a man with a mission," Bentley mused.

"Just finished one. That young man will never want to lift a video game again."

"Good for you. Didn't arrest him?"

Kilraven arched an eyebrow. "Actually he knows some cheat codes for 'Call of Duty' that even I haven't worked out. So I called our police chief."

"Cheat codes are against the law?" Cappie asked, puzzled.

Kilraven chuckled. "No. Cash has a young

brother-in-law, Rory, who's nuts about 'Call of Duty,' so our potential shoplifter is going to go over to Cash's house later and teach them to him. Cash may have a few words to add to the ones I gave him."

"Neat strategy," Bentley said.

Kilraven shrugged. "The boy loves gaming but he lives with a widowed mother who works two jobs just to keep food on the table. He wanted 'Call of Duty,' but he didn't have any money. If he and Rory hit it off, and I think they might, he'll get to play the game and learn model citizen habits on the side."

"Good psychology," Bentley told him.

Kilraven sighed. "It's tough on kids, having an economy like this. Gaming is a way of life for the younger generation, but those game consoles and games for them are expensive."

"That's why we have a whole table of used games that are more affordable," the owner of the store, overhearing them, commented with a grin. "Thanks, Kilraven."

The officer shrugged. "I spend so much time in here that I feel obliged to protect the merchandise," he commented.

The store owner patted him on the back. "Good

man. I might give you a discount on your next sale."

Kilraven glared at him. "Attempting to bribe a police officer…"

The owner held up both hands. "I never!" he exclaimed. "I said 'might'!"

Kilraven grinned. "Thanks, though. It was a nice thought. You wouldn't have any games based on Scottish history?" he added.

The store owner, a tall, handsome young man, gave him a pitying look. "Listen, you're the only customer I've ever had who likes sixteenth-century Scottish history. And I'll tell you again that most historians think James Hepburn got what he deserved."

"He did not," Kilraven muttered. "Lord Bothwell was led astray by that French-thinking Queen. Her wiles did him in."

"Wiles?" Cappie asked, wide-eyed. "What are wiles?"

"If you have to ask, you don't have any," Bentley said helpfully.

She laughed. "Okay. Fair enough."

Kilraven shook his head. "Bothwell had admirable qualities," he insisted, staring at the shop owner. "He was utterly fearless, could read and

write and speak French, and even his worst enemies said that he was incapable of being bribed."

"Which may be, but still doesn't provide grounds
for a video game," the manager replied.

Kilraven pointed a finger at him. "Just because
you're a partisan of Mary, Queen of Scots, is no
reason to take issue with her Lord High Admiral.
And I should point out that there's no video game
about her, either!"

"Hooray," the manager murmured dryly. "Oh,
look, a customer!" He took the opportunity to vanish toward the counter.

Kilraven's two companions were giving him
odd looks.

"Entertainment should be educational," he defended himself.

"It is," Bentley pointed out. "In this game—"
he held up a Star Trek one "—you can learn how
to shoot down enemy ships. And in this one—"
he held up a comical one about aliens "—you can
learn to use a death ray and blow up buildings."

"You have no appreciation of true history," Kilraven sighed. "I should have taught it in grammar
school."

"I can see you now, standing in front of the
school board, explaining why the kids were hav-

ing nightmares about sixteenth-century interrogation techniques," Bentley mused.

Kilraven pursed his lips. "I myself have been accused of using those," he said. "Can you believe it? I mean, I'm such a law-abiding citizen and all."

"I can think of at least one potential kidnapper who might disagree," Bentley commented.

"Lies. Vicious lies," he said defensively. "He got those bruises from trying to squeeze through a car window."

"While it was going sixty miles an hour, I believe?" the other man queried.

"Hey, it's not my fault he didn't want to wait for the arraignment."

"Good thing you noticed the window was cracked in time."

"Yes," Kilraven sighed. "Sad, though, that I didn't realize he had a blackjack. He gave it to me very politely, though."

Bentley glanced at Cappie. "Was it a sprained wrist or a fractured one?" he wondered.

Kilraven gave him a cold glare. "It was a figment."

"A what?"

"Of his imagination," Kilraven assured him. He chuckled. "Anyway, he's going to be in jail for a long time. The resisting arrest charge, added to assault on a police officer, makes two felony charges in addition to the kidnapping ones."

"I hope you never get mad at me," Bentley said.

"I'd worry more about the chief," Kilraven replied. "He fed a guy a soapy sponge in front of the whole neighborhood."

"He was provoked, I hear," Bentley said.

"A felon verbally assaulted him in his own yard while he was washing his car. Of course, Cash has mellowed since his marriage."

"Not much," Bentley said. "And he's still pretty good with a sniper kit. Saved Colby Lane's little girl when she was kidnapped."

"He practices on Eb Scott's firing range," Kilraven said. "We all do. He lets us use it free. State-of-the-art stuff, computers and everything."

"Eb Scott?" Cappie asked.

"Eb was a merc," Kilraven told her. "He and Cy Parks and Micah Steele fought in some of the bloodiest wars in Africa a few years back. They're all married and somewhat settled. But like Cash Grier, they're not really tame."

Cappie only nodded. She was recalling what her brother had said about Cy Parks.

Kilraven cleared his throat. "Oops, lunchtime is over. I've got to go. See you."

"You didn't have lunch," Bentley observed.

"I had a big breakfast," Kilraven replied. "Can't waste my lunch hour eating," he added with a grin. "See you."

"Imagine him, a gamer," Cappie commented. "I'd never have thought it."

"A lot of military men keep their hand-eye coordination skills sharp playing them," he said.

"Were you in the military?" Cappie wanted to know.

He smiled and nodded. "I have it on good authority that it's all that saved me from a life of crime. I got picked up for hanging around with a couple of bad kids who knocked over a drugstore. I was just in the car with them, but I got charged with a felony." He sighed. "My mother went to the judge and promised him her next child if he'd let me join the army instead of standing trial. He agreed." He glanced down at her with a smile. "He's in his seventies now, but I still send him a Christmas present every year. I owe him."

"That was nice."

"I thought so, too."

"Kell got into some trouble in his senior year of high school. I don't remember it, I was so young, but he told me about it. He was hanging out with one of the inner-city gangs and there was a firefight. He didn't get shot, but one of the boys in the gang was killed. Kell got arrested right along with them. He drew a female judge who had grown up in gang territory and lost a brother to the violence. She gave him a choice of facing trial or going into the service and making something of his life. He took her at her word, and made her proud." She sighed. "It was tragic, about her. She was shot and killed in her own living room during a drug deal shootout next door."

"Life is dangerous," Bentley remarked.

She nodded. "Unpredictable and dangerous." She looked up at him. "I guess maybe that's why I like playing video games. They give me something that I can control. Life is never that way."

He smiled. "No. It isn't." He watched as she took a copy of "Halo: ODST" off the shelf. "Going to make him wait until Christmas to play it?"

"Yes."

His eyes twinkled. "I could bring my copy over. Let you get a taste of it before the fact."

She looked fascinated. "You could?"

"Ask Kell." He hesitated. "I could bring a pizza with me. And some beer."

She pursed her lips. "I'm already drooling." She grimaced. "I could cook something…"

"Not fair. You shouldn't have to provide for guests. Besides, I haven't had a decent pizza in weeks. I'll be on call tonight, but we might get lucky."

Her eyes brightened. "That would be nice. I'm sure Kell would enjoy it. We don't get much company."

"About six?"

Her heart jumped. "Yes. About six would be fine."

"It's a date."

"I'll see you then."

He nodded.

She walked, a little wobbly, to the counter and paid for her game. Her life had just changed in a heartbeat. She didn't know where it would lead, and she was a little nervous about getting involved with her boss. But he was very nice-looking and he had qualities that she admired. Besides, she thought, it was just a night of gaming. Nothing suspect about that.

SHE TOLD KELL the minute she got home.

He laughed. "Don't look so guilty," he chided. "I like your boss. Besides, it's neat to see the game I might get for Christmas." He smiled angelically.

"You might get it," she said, "and you might not."

"You might get a new raincoat," he mused.

She grinned. "Wow."

He looked at her fondly. "It's hard, living like this, I know. We were better off in San Antonio. But I didn't want us to be around when Frank got out of jail." His face hardened.

Her heart jumped. She hadn't thought about Frank for several days in a row. But now the trial and his fury came back, full force. "It was almost six months ago that he was arrested, and three months until the trial. He got credit for time served. We've been here just about three months." She bit her lower lip. "Oh, dear. They'll let him out pretty soon."

His pale eyes were cold. "It should have been a tougher sentence. But despite his past, it was the first time he was ever charged with battery, and they couldn't get more jail time for him on a first offense. The public defender in his case was pretty talented, as well."

She drew in a long breath. "I'm glad we're out of the city."

"So am I. He lived barely a block from us. We're not as easy to get to, here."

She stared at him closely. "You believe the threats he made," she murmured. "Don't you?"

"He's the sort of man who gets even," he told her. "I'm not the man I was, or we'd never have left town on the chance he might come after you. But here, I have friends. If he comes down here looking for trouble, he'll find some."

She felt a little better. "I didn't want to have him arrested again."

"It wouldn't have mattered," he told her. "The fact that you stood up to him was enough. He was used to women being afraid of him. His own sister sat in the back of the courtroom during the trial. She was afraid to get near him, because she hadn't lied for him when the police came."

"What makes a man like that?" she asked sadly. "What makes him so hard that he has to beat up a woman to make him feel strong?"

"I don't know, sis," Kell told her gently. "Honestly I don't think the man has feelings for anybody or anything. His sister told you that he threw her dog off a bridge when they were kids. He laughed about it."

Her face grew sad. "I thought he was such a gentleman. He was so sweet to me, bringing me flowers and candy at work, writing me love letters. Then he came over to our house and the first thing he did was kick my cat when it spit at him."

"The cat was a good judge of character," Kell remarked.

"When I protested, he said that animals didn't

feel pain and I shouldn't get so worked up over a stupid cat. I should have realized then what sort of person he was."

"People in love are neither sane nor responsible," Kell replied flatly. "You were so crazy about him that I think you could have forgiven murder."

She nodded sadly. "I learned the hard way that looks and acts are no measure of a man. I should have run for my life the first time he phoned me at work just to talk."

"You didn't know. How could you? He was a stranger."

"You knew," she said.

He nodded. "I've known men like him in the service," he said. "They're good in combat, because they aren't bothered by the carnage. But that trait serves them poorly in civilian life."

She cocked her head at him. "Kilraven said that Eb Scott lets law enforcement use his gun range for free. Don't you know him, too?"

"Yes."

"And Micah Steele."

"Yes."

She hesitated. "They're all retired mercenaries, Kell."

"So they are."

"Were they involved with the military?" she persisted.

"The military uses contract personnel," he said evasively. "People with necessary skills for certain jobs."

"Like combat."

"Exactly," he replied. "We used certain firms to supplement our troops overseas in the Middle East. They're used in Africa for certain covert operations."

"So much secrecy," she complained.

"Well, you don't advertise something that might get you sued or cause a diplomatic upheaval," he pointed out. "Covert ops have always been a part of the military. Even what they call transparency in government is never going to threaten that. As long as we have renegade states that threaten our sovereignty, we'll have black ops." He glanced at the clock. "Shouldn't you warm up the game system?" he asked. "It's five-thirty."

"Already?" she exclaimed. "Goodness, I need to tidy up the living room! And the kitchen. He's bringing pizza and beer!"

"You don't drink," he said.

"Well, no, but you like a beer now and then. I expect somebody told him." She flushed.

"I do like a glass of beer." He smiled. "It's also nice to have friends who provide food."

"Like your friend Cy and the Chinese stuff. I'll get spoiled."

"Maybe that's the idea. Your boss likes you."

She'd gotten that idea, herself. "Don't mention horns, pitchforks or breathing fire while he's here," she said firmly.

He saluted her.

She made a face at him and went to do her chores.

"THAT'S NOT FAIR!" Cappie burst out when she'd "died" for the tenth time trying to take out one of the Hunters in the Halo game.

"Don't throw the controller," Kell said firmly.

She had it by one lobe, gripped tightly. She grimaced and slowly lowered it. "Okay," she said. "But they do bounce, and they're almost shockproof."

"She ought to know," Kell told an amused Bentley Rydel. "She's bounced it off the walls several times in recent weeks."

"Well, they keep killing me!" she burst out. "It's not my fault! These Hunters aren't like the ones in 'Halo 3...' They're almost invincible, and there are so many of them...!"

"I'd worry more about the alien grunts that keep taking you out with sticky grenades," Bentley pointed out. "While you're trying to snipe the Hunters, the little guys are blowing you up right and left."

"I want a flame thrower," she wailed. "Or a rocket launcher! Why can't I find a rocket launcher?"

"We wouldn't want to make it too easy, now would we?" Bentley chided. He smiled at her fury. "Patience. You have to go slow and take them on one at a time, so they don't flank you."

She gave her boss a speaking look, turned back to the screen and tried again.

IT WAS LATE when he left. The three of them had taken turns on the controller. Bentley and Kell had wanted to try the split screen, but that would have put Cappie right out of the competition, because she was only comfortable playing by herself.

She walked Bentley outside. "Thanks for bringing the pizza and beer," she said. "Some other time, I'd like to have you over for supper, if you'd like. I can cook."

He smiled. "I'll take you up on that. I can cook, too, but I only know how to do a few things from scratch. It gets tiresome after a while."

"Thanks for bringing the game over, too," she added. "It's really good. Kell is going to love it."

"What did we all do for entertainment before video games?" he wondered aloud as they reached his car.

"I used to watch game shows," she said. "Kell liked police dramas and old movies."

"I like some of the forensic shows, but I almost never get to see a whole one," he sighed. "There's always an emergency. It's always a large animal call. And since I'm the only vet on staff who does large animal calls, it's always me."

"Yes, but you never complain, not even if it's sleeting out," she said gently.

He smiled. "I like my clients."

"They like you, too." She shook her head. "Amazing, isn't it?"

"Excuse me?"

She flushed. "Oh, no, not because of...I mean..." She grimaced. "I meant it's amazing that you never get tired of large animal calls when the weather's awful."

He chuckled. "You really have got to take an assertiveness course," he said, and not unkindly.

"It's hard to be assertive when you're shy," she argued.

"It's impossible not to be when you have a job

like mine and people don't want to do what you tell them to," he returned. "Some animals would die if I couldn't outargue their owners."

"Point taken."

"If it's any consolation," he said, "when I was your age, I had the same problem."

"How did you overcome it?"

"My stepfather decided that my mother wasn't going to the doctor for a urinary tract infection. I was already in veterinary school, and I knew what happened when animals weren't treated for it. I told him. He told me he was the man of the house and he'd decide what my mother did." He smiled, remembering. "So I had a choice—either back down, or let my mother risk permanent damage to her health, even death. I told him she was going to the doctor, I put her in the car and drove her there myself."

"What did your stepfather do?" she asked, aghast.

"There wasn't much that he could do, since I paid the doctor." His face hardened. "And it wasn't the first disagreement we'd had. He was poor and proud with it. He'd have let her suffer rather than admit he couldn't afford a doctor visit or medicine." He looked down at her. "It's a hell of a world, when people have to choose between food and medicine and doctors. Or between heated houses and medicine."

"Tell me about it," she replied. She colored a little, and hoped he didn't notice. "Kell and I do all right," she said quickly. "But he'll go without medicine sometimes if I don't put my foot down. You'd think I'd be tough as nails, because I stand up to him."

"He's not a mean person."

"He could be, I think," she said. She hesitated. "There was a man I dated, briefly, in San Antonio." She hesitated again. Perhaps it was too soon for this.

He stepped closer. "A man."

His voice was very soft. Quiet. Comforting. She wrapped her arms around her chest. She had on a sweater, but it was chilly outside. The memories were just as chilling. She was recalling it, her face betraying her inner turmoil. He'd hit her. The first time, he said it was because he'd had a drink, and he cried, and she went back to him. But the second time, he'd have probably killed her if Kell hadn't heard her scream and come to save her. As it was, he'd fractured her arm when he threw her over the couch. Kell had knocked Frank out with a lamp, from his wheelchair, and made her call the police.

He made her testify, too. She held her arms around herself, chilled by the memory.

"What happened?"

She looked up at him, wanting to tell him, but afraid to. Frank got a six-month sentence, but he'd already served three months and he was out. Would he come after her now? Would he be crazy enough to do that? And would Bentley believe her, if she told him? They barely knew each other. It was too soon, she thought. Much too soon, to drag out her past and show it to him. There was no reason to tell him anyway. Frank wouldn't come down here and risk being sent back to jail. Bentley might think less of her if she told him, might think it was her own fault. Besides, she didn't want to tell him yet.

"HE WAS A mean sort of person, that's all," she hedged. "He kicked my cat. I thought it was terrible. He just laughed."

His blue eyes narrowed. "A man who'll kick a cat will kick a human being."

"You're probably right," she admitted, and then she smiled. "Well, I only dated him for a little while. He wasn't the sort of person I like to be around. Kell didn't like him, either."

"I like your brother."

She smiled. "I like him, too. He was just going downhill with depression in San Antonio. We were over our ears in debt, from all the hospital bills. It's lucky our cousin died and left us this place," she added.

Bentley's eyebrows lifted. "This place belonged to Harry Farley. He got killed overseas in the military about six months ago. He didn't have any relatives at all. The county buried him, out of respect for his military service."

"But Kell said…" she blurted out.

Her expression made Bentley hesitate. "Oh. Wait a minute," Bentley said at once. "That's right, I did hear that he had a distant cousin or two."

She laughed. "That's us."

"My mistake. I wasn't thinking." He studied her quietly. "Well, I guess I'd better go. This is the first Saturday night I can remember when I didn't get called out," he added with a smile. "Pure dumb luck, I guess."

"Law of averages," she countered. "You have to get lucky sooner or later."

"I guess. I'll see you Monday."

"Thanks again for the pizza."

He opened the door of the Land Rover. "I'll take you up on the offer of supper," he said. "When we set a date, you can tell me what you want to fix and I'll bring the raw ingredients." He held up a hand when she started to protest. "It does no good to argue with me. You can't win. Just ask Keely. Better yet, ask Dr. King," he chuckled.

She laughed, too. "Okay, then."

"Good night."

"Good night."

He closed the door behind him. Cappie went back up on the porch and watched him throw up a hand as he drove away. She stood there for several seconds before she realized that the wind was chilling her. She went in, feeling happier than she had in a long time.

CHAPTER FIVE

CAPPIE FELT AWKWARD with Bentley the following
Monday. She wasn't sure if she should mention
that he'd been to her house over the weekend. Her
coworkers were very nice, but she was nervous
when she thought they might tease her about the
doctor. That would never do. She didn't want to
make him feel uncomfortable in his own office.

Having lived so long in San Antonio, she didn't
know about life in small towns. It hadn't occurred
to her that nothing that happened could be kept
secret.

"How was the pizza?" Dr. King asked her.

Cappie stared at her in horror.

Dr. King grinned. "My cousin works at the
pizza place. Dr. Rydel mentioned where he was
taking it. And she's best friends with Art, who
runs the software store, so she knew he was taking
the game over to play with you and your brother."

"Oh, dear," Cappie said worriedly.

Dr. King patted her on the back. "There, there," she said in a comforting tone. "You'll get used to it. We're like a big family in Jacobs County, because most of us have lived here all our lives, and our families have lived here for generations, mostly. We know everything that's going on. We only read the newspaper to find out who got caught doing it."

"Oh, dear," Cappie said again.

"Hi," Keely said, removing her coat as she joined them. "How was the game Saturday?" she added.

Cappie looked close to tears.

Dr. King gave Keely a speaking glance. "She's not used to small towns yet," she explained.

"Not to worry," Keely told her. "Dr. Rydel certainly is." She laughed at Cappie's tormented expression. "If he was worried about gossip, you'd better believe he'd never have put a foot inside your door."

"She thinks we'll tease her," Dr. King said.

"Not a chance," Keely added. "We were all dating somebody once." She flushed. "Especially me, and very recently." She meant her husband, Boone, of course.

"And nobody teased her," Dr. King added. "Well," she qualified it, "not where Boone could hear it, anyway," she added and chuckled.

"Thanks," she said.

Dr. King just smiled. "You know, Bentley hates most women. One of our younger clients made a play for him one day. She wore suggestive clothing and a lot of makeup and when he leaned over to examine her dog, she kissed him."

Cappie's eyes widened. "What did he do?"

"He left the room, dragged me in there and told the young lady that he was indisposed and Dr. King would be handling the case."

"What did the young lady do?" Cappie asked.

"Turned red as a beet, picked up her dog and left the building. It turns out," Dr. King added with a grin, "that the dog was in excellent health. She only used it as an excuse to get Dr. Rydel in there with her."

"Did she come back?"

"Oh, yes, she was an extremely persistent young woman. The third time she showed up here, she insisted on seeing Dr. Rydel. He called Cash Grier, our police chief, and had him come in and explain the legal ramifications of sexual harassment to the young lady. He didn't smile while he was speaking. And when he finished talking, the young lady took her animal, went home and subsequently moved back to Dallas."

"Well!" Cappie exclaimed.

"So you see, Dr. Rydel is quite capable of deterring unwanted interest." She leaned closer. "I understand that you like to play video games?"

Cappie laughed. "Yes, I do."

"My husband has a score of over 16,000 on Xbox LIVE," she said, and wiggled her eyebrows.

Keely was staring at her, uncomprehending.

"My scores are around 4,000," Cappie said helpfully. "And my brother's are about 15,000." She chuckled. "The higher the score, the better the player. Also, the more often the playing."

"I guess my score would be around 200," Dr. King sighed. "You see, I get called in a lot for emergencies when Dr. Rydel is out on large animal calls. So I start a lot of games that my husband gets to finish."

"Kell had buddies in the army who could outdo even those scores. Those guys were great!" Cappie said. "They'd hang out with us when they were off duty. Kell always had nice video gaming equipment. Some of them did, too, but we always had a full fridge. Boy, could those guys eat!"

"You lived overseas a lot, didn't you?" Keely asked.

"Yes. I've seen a lot of exotic places."

"What was your favorite?"

"Japan," Cappie replied at once, smiling. "We went there when Kell was stationed in Korea. Not that Korea isn't a beautiful country. But I really loved Japan. You should see the gaming equipment they've got. And the cell phone technology." She shook her head. "They're really a long way ahead of us in technology."

"Did you get to ride the bullet train?" Keely asked.

"Yes. It's as fast as they say it is. I loved the train station. I loved everything! Kyoto was like a living painting. So many gardens and trees and temples."

"I'd love to see any city in Japan, but especially Kyoto," Keely said. "Judd Dunn's wife, Christabel, went over there with him to buy beef. She said Kyoto was just unbelievable. So much history, and so beautiful."

"It is," Cappie replied. "We got to visit a temple. The Zen garden was so stark, and so lovely. It's just sand and rocks, you know. The sand is raked into patterns like water. The rocks are situated like land. All around were Japanese black pine trees and bamboo trees as tall as the pines, with huge trunks. There was a bamboo forest, all green, and a huge pond full of Japanese Koi fish." She shook her head. "You know, I could live there. Kell said it was his favorite, too, of all the places we lived."

"Are we going to work today, or travel around the world?" came a deep, curt voice from behind them.

Everybody jumped. "Sorry, Dr. Rydel," Keely said at once.

"Me, too," Cappie seconded.

"Nihongo no daisuki desu," Dr. Rydel said, and made a polite bow.

Cappie burst out smiling. *"Nihon no tomodachi desu. Konichi wa, Rydel sama,"* she replied, and bowed back.

Keely and Dr. King stared at them, fascinated.

"I said that I liked Japanese language," Dr. Rydel translated.

"And I said that I was a friend of Japan. I also told him hello," Cappie seconded. "You speak Japanese!" she exclaimed to Bentley.

"Just enough to get me arrested in Tokyo," Bentley told her, smiling. "I was stationed in Okinawa when I was in the service. I spent my liberties in Tokyo."

"Well, isn't it a small world?" Dr. King wondered.

"Small, and very crowded," Bentley told her. He gave her a meaningful look. "If you don't believe me, you could look at the mob in the waiting room, glaring at the empty reception counter and pointedly staring at their watches."

"Oops!" Dr. King ran for it.

So did Keely and Cappie, laughing all the way.

THERE WAS A new rapport between Dr. Rydel and Cappie. He was no longer antagonistic toward her, and she wasn't afraid of him anymore. Their working relationship became cordial, almost friendly.

Then he came to supper the following Saturday, and she found herself dropping pots and pans and getting tongue-tied at the table while the three of them ate the meal she'd painstakingly prepared.

"You're a very good cook," Bentley told her, smiling.

"Thanks," she replied, flushing even more.

Kell, watching her, was amused and indulgent. "She could cook even when she was in her early teens," he told Bentley. "Of course, that was desperation," he added with a sigh.

She laughed. "He can burn water," she pointed out. "I had so much carbon in my diet that I felt like a fire drill. I borrowed a cookbook from the wife of one of his buddies and started practicing. She felt sorry for me and gave me lessons."

"They were delicious lessons," Kell recalled with a smile. "The woman was a *cordon bleu* cook and she could make French pastries. I gained ten pounds. Then her husband was reassigned and the lessons stopped."

"Hey, a new family moved in," she argued. "It was a company commander, and she could make these terrific vegan dishes."

Kell glared at her. "I hate vegetables."

"Different strokes for different folks," she shot back. "Besides, there's nothing wrong with a good squash casserole."

Kell and Bentley exchanged horrified looks.

"What is it with men and squash?" she exclaimed, throwing up her hands. "I have never met a man who would eat squash in any form. It's a perfectly respectable vegetable. You can make all sorts of things with it."

Bentley pursed his lips. "Door props, paperweights…"

"Food things!" she returned.

"Hey, I don't eat paperweights," Bentley pointed out.

She shook her head.

"Why don't you bring in that terrific dessert you made?" Kell prompted.

"I guess I could do that," she told him. She got up and started gathering plates. Bentley got up and helped, as naturally as if he'd done it all his life.

She gave him an odd look.

"I live alone." He shrugged. "I'm used to clearing the table." He frowned. "Well, throwing away plastic plates, anyway. I eat a lot of TV dinners."

She made a face.

"There is nothing wrong with a TV dinner," Kell added. "I've eaten my share of them."

"Only when I was working late and it was all you could get," Cappie laughed. "And mostly, I left you things that you could just microwave."

"Point conceded." Kell grinned.

"What sort of dessert did you make?" Bentley asked.

She laughed. "A pound cake."

He whistled. "I haven't tasted one of those in years. My mother used to make them." His pleasant expression drained away for a few seconds.

Cappie knew he was remembering his mother's death. "It's a chocolate pound cake," she said, smiling, as she tried to draw him out of the past.

"Even better," he said, smiling. "Those are rare. Barbara sells slices of one sometimes at her café, but not too often."

"A lot of people can't eat chocolate, on account of allergies," she said.

"I don't have allergies," Bentley assured her. "And I do hope it's a large pound cake. If you offered to send a slice home with me, I might let you come in an hour late one day next week."

"Why, Dr. Rydel, that sounds suspiciously like a bribe," she exclaimed.

He grinned. "It is."

"In that case, you can take home two slices," she said.

He chuckled.

Watching them head into the kitchen, Kell smiled to himself. Cappie had been afraid of men just after her bad experience with the date from hell. It was good to see her comfortable in a man's company. Bentley might be just the man to heal her emotional scars.

"Where do you want these?" Bentley asked when he'd scraped the plates.

"Just put them in the sink. I'll clean up in here later."

He looked around quietly. The kitchen was bare bones. There was an older microwave oven, an old stove and refrigerator, a table and chairs that looked as if they'd come from a yard sale. The coffeepot and Crock-Pot on the counter had seen better days.

She noticed his interest and smiled sadly. "We didn't bring a lot of stuff with us when we moved back to San Antonio. We sold a lot of things to other servicemen so we wouldn't have to pay the moving costs. Then, after Kell got wounded, we sold more stuff so we could afford to pay the rent."

"Didn't he have any medical insurance?"

She shook her head. "He said there was some sort of mix-up with the magazine's insurer, and he got left out in the cold." She removed the cover from the cake pan and got out cake plates to serve it on. Her mother's small china service had been one thing she'd managed to salvage. She loved the pretty rose pattern.

"That's too bad," Bentley murmured. But he was frowning behind her, his keen mind on some things he recalled about her mysterious brother. If Kell was friendly with the local mercs, it was unlikely he'd gotten to know them in the military. They were too old to have served anytime recently. But he did know that they'd been in Africa in recent years. So had Kell. That was more than a coincidence, he was almost sure.

His silence made her curious. She turned around, her soft eyes wide and searching.

His own pale blue eyes narrowed on her pretty face in its frame of long blond hair. She had a pert little figure, enhanced by the white sweater and blue jeans she was wearing. Her breasts were firm and small, just right for her build. He felt his whole body clench at the way she was looking at him.

He wasn't handsome, she was thinking, but he had a killer physique, from his powerful long legs in blue jeans to his broad chest outlined under the knit shirt. Beige suited his coloring, made his tan look bronzed, the turtleneck enhancing his strong throat.

"You're staring," he pointed out huskily.

She searched for the right words. Her mouth was dry. "Your ears have very nice lobes."

He blinked. "Excuse me?"

She flushed to her hairline. "Oh, good heavens!" She fumbled with the cake knife and it started to fall. He stepped forward and caught it halfway to the floor, just as she dived for it. They collided.

His arm slid around her to prevent her from going headlong into the counter and pulled her up short, right against him. Her intake of breath was audible as she clung to him to keep her footing.

She felt his chin against her temple, heard his breath coming out raggedly. His arm contracted.

"Th…thanks," she managed to say against his throat. "I'm just so clumsy sometimes!"

"Nobody's perfect."

She laughed nervously. "Certainly not me. Thanks for saving the cake knife."

"My pleasure."

His voice was almost a purr, deep and soft and slow. He lifted his head very slowly, so that his eyes were suddenly looking right into hers. She felt his chest rise and fall against her breasts in an intimacy that grew more smoldering by the second. She looked up, but her eyes stopped at his chiseled mouth. It was very sensuous. She'd never really paid it much attention, until now. And she couldn't quite stop looking at it.

She felt his fingers curling into her long hair, as if he loved the feel of it.

"I love long hair," he said softly. "Yours is beautiful."

"Thanks," she whispered.

"Soft hair. Pretty mouth." He bent and his nose slid against hers as his mouth poised over her parted lips. "Very pretty mouth."

She stood very still, waiting, hoping that he wasn't going to draw back. She loved the way his body felt, so close to hers. She loved his strength, his height, the spicy scent of his cologne. She hung there, at his lips, her eyes half closed, waiting, waiting...

"Where's that cake?" came a plaintive cry from the living room. "I'm starving!"

They jumped apart so quickly that Cappie almost fell. "Coming right up!" Heavens, was that her voice? It sounded almost artificial!

"I'll take the coffeepot into the living room for you," Bentley said. His own voice was oddly hoarse and deep, and he didn't look at her as he went out of the room.

Cappie cut the cake, forcing her mind to ignore what had almost happened. She had so many complications in her life right now that she didn't really need another one. But she did wonder if it was possible to put this particular genie back in its bottle.

AND, IN FACT, it wasn't. When they finished the cake and a few more minutes of conversation, Bentley got a call from his answering service and hung up with a grimace.

"One of Cy Parks's purebred heifers is calving for the first time. I'll have to go. Sorry. I really enjoyed the meal, and the cake."

"So did we," Cappie said.

"We'll have to do this again," Kell added, grinning.

"Next time, I'll take the two of you out to a nice restaurant," Bentley said.

"Well…" Cappie hesitated.

"Walk me out," Bentley told her, and he didn't smile.

Cappie looked toward Kell to save her, but he only grinned. She turned and followed Bentley out the door.

He paused at the steps, looking down at her with a long, unblinking stare in the faint light that shone out from the windows.

She bit her lower lip and searched for something to say. Her mind wouldn't cooperate.

He couldn't seem to find anything to say, either. They just stared at each other.

"I hate women," he bit off.

She faltered. "I'm sorry," she said.

"Oh, what the hell. Come here."

He scooped her up against him, bent his head and kissed her with such immediate passion that she couldn't even think. Her arms went around his neck as she warmed to the hard, insistent pressure of his mouth as it parted her lips and invaded the soft, secret warmth of her mouth. It was too much, too soon, but she couldn't say that. He didn't leave her enough breath to say anything, and the pleasure throbbing through her body robbed her mind of the words, anyway.

Seconds later, he put her back on her feet and moved away. "Well!" he said huskily.

She stared up at him with her mouth open.

His eyebrows arched.

She tried to speak, but she couldn't manage a single word.

He let out a rough breath. "I really wish you wouldn't look at me in that tone of voice," he said.

"Wh…what?" she stammered.

He chuckled softly. "Well, I could say I'm flattered that I leave you speechless, but I won't embarrass you. See you Monday."

She nodded. "Monday."

"At the office."

She nodded again. "The office."

"Cappie?"

She was still staring at him. She nodded once more. "Cappie."

He burst out laughing. He bent and kissed her again. "And they say the way to a man's heart is through his stomach," he mused. "This is much quicker than food. See you."

He turned and went to his car. Cappie stood and watched him until he was all the way to the main highway. It wasn't until Kell called to her that she realized it was cold and she didn't even have on a coat.

AFTER THAT, IT was hard to work in the same office with Bentley without staring at him, starstruck, when she saw him in between patients. He noticed. He couldn't seem to stop smiling. But when Cappie started running into door facings looking at him, everybody else in the office started grinning, and that did inhibit her.

She forced herself to keep her mind on the animal patients, and not the tall man who was treating them.

Just before quitting time, a little boy came careening into the practice just ahead of a man. He was carrying a big dog, wrapped in a blanket, shivering and bleeding.

"Please, it's my dog, you have to help him!" the boy sobbed.

A worried man joined him. "He was hit by a

car," the man said. "The so-and-so didn't even stop! He just kept going!"

Dr. Rydel came out of the back and took a quick look at the dog. "Bring him right back," he told the boy. He managed a smile. "We'll do everything we can. I promise."

"His name's Ben," the boy sobbed. "I've had him since I was little. He's my best friend."

Dr. Bentley helped the boy lift Ben onto the metal operating table. He didn't ask the boy to leave while he did the examination. He had Keely help him clean the wound and help restrain the dog while he assessed the damage. "We're going to need an X-ray. Get Billy to help you carry him," he told her with a smile.

"Yes, sir."

"Is he going to die?" the boy wailed.

Dr. Rydel put a kindly hand on his shoulder. "I don't see any evidence of internal damage or concussion. It looks like a fracture, but before I can reduce it, I'm going to need to do X-rays to see the extent of the damage. Then we'll do blood work to make sure it's safe to anesthetize him. I will have to operate. He has some skin and muscle damage in addition to the fracture."

The man with the boy looked worried. "Is this going to be expensive?" he asked worriedly.

The boy wailed.

"I lost my job last week," the man said heavily. "We've got a new baby."

"Don't worry about it," Dr. Rydel said in a reassuring tone. "We do some pro bono work here, and I'm overdue. We'll take care of it."

The man bit his lower lip, hard, and averted his eyes. "Thanks," he gritted.

"We all have rough patches," Dr. Rydel told him. "We get through them. It will get better."

"Thanks, Doc!" the boy burst out, reaching over to rub a worried hand over the old dog's head. "Thanks!"

"I like dogs, myself," the doctor chuckled. "Now this is going to take a while. Why don't you leave your phone number at the desk and I'll call you as soon as your dog's through surgery?"

"You'd do that?" the man asked, surprised.

"Of course. We always do that."

"His name's Ben," the boy said, sniffing. "He's had all his shots and stuff. We take him every year to the clinic at the animal shelter."

Which meant money was always tight, but they took care of the animal. Dr. Rydel was impressed.

"We'll give her our phone number. You're a good man," the boy's father said quietly.

"I like dogs," Dr. Rydel said again with a smile. "Go on home. We'll call you."

"You be good, Ben," the boy told his dog, petting him one last time. The dog wasn't even trying to bite anybody. He whined a little. "We'll come and get you just as soon as we can. Honest."

The man tugged the boy along with him, giving the vet one last grateful smile.

"I can take care of his bill," Keely volunteered.

Dr. Rydel shook his head. "I do it in extreme cases like this. It's no hardship."

"Yes, but..."

He leaned closer. "I drive a Land Rover. Want to price one?"

Keely burst out laughing. "Okay. I give up."

Billy, the vet tech, came to help Keely get Ben in to X-ray. Cappie came back after a minute. "I promised I'd make sure you knew that Ben likes peanut butter," she said. "Who's Ben?"

"Fractured leg, HBC," he abbreviated.

She smiled. "Hit by car," she translated. "The most frequent injury suffered by dogs. They know who hit him?"

"I wish," Dr. Rydel said fervently. "I'd call Cash Grier myself."

"They didn't stop?"

"No," he said shortly.

"I'd stop, if I hit somebody's pet," Cappie said gently. "I had a cat, when we lived in San Antonio, after Kell got out of the army. I had to give him away when we moved down here." She was remembering that Frank had kicked him, so hard that Cappie took him to work with her the next day, just to have him checked out. He had bruising, but, fortunately, no broken bones. Then the cat had run away, and returned after Frank was gone. She'd given the cat away before she and Kell left town, to make sure that Frank wouldn't send somebody to get even with her by hurting her cat. He was that sort of man.

"You're very pensive," he commented.

"I was missing my cat," she lied, smiling.

"We have lots of cats around here," he told her. "I think Keely has a whole family of them out in her barn and there are new kittens. She'd give you one, if you asked."

She hesitated. "I'm not sure if I could keep a cat," she replied. "Kell wouldn't be able to look out for him, you know. He has all he can do to take care of himself."

He didn't push. He just smiled. "One day, he'll meet some nice girl who'll want to take him home with her and spoil him rotten."

She blinked. "Kell?"

"Why not? He's only paralyzed, you know, not demented."

She laughed. "I guess not. He's pretty tough."

"And he's not a bad gamer, either," he pointed out.

"I noticed."

"Cappie, have you got the charges for Miss Dill's cat in here yet?" came a call from the front counter.

She grimaced. "No, sorry, Dr. King. I'll be right there."

She rushed back out, flustered. Dr. Rydel certainly had a way of looking at her that increased her heart rate. She liked it, too.

CHAPTER SIX

CAPPIE STAYED LATE to help with the overflow of patients, held up by the emergency surgery on the dog. The practice generally did its scheduled surgeries on Thursdays, but emergencies were always accommodated. In fact, there was a twenty-four-hour-a-day emergency service up in San Antonio, but the veterinarians at Dr. Rydel's practice would always come in if they were needed. In certain instances, the long drive to the big city would have meant the death of a furry patient. They were considering the addition of a fourth veterinarian to the practice, so that they could more easily accommodate those emergencies.

The dog, Ben, came out of surgery with a mended foreleg and was placed in a recovery cage to wait until the anesthetic wore off. The next day, if he presented no complications, he would be sent home with antibiotics, painkillers and detailed instructions on post-surgical care. Cappie was glad, for the boy's sake. She felt sorriest for the children whose pets were injured. Not that grown-up people took those situations any easier. Pets were like part of the family. It was hard to see one hurt, or to lose one.

Kell was pensive when she got home. In fact, he looked broody. She put down her coat and purse. "What's the matter with you?" she asked with a grin.

He put his laptop computer aside with deliberation. "I had a call from an assistant district attorney's office in San Antonio, from the victim support people," he said quietly. "Frank Bartlett got out of jail today."

It was the day she'd been dreading. Her heart sank. He'd vowed revenge. He would make her pay, he said, for having him tried and convicted.

"Don't worry," he added gently. "We're among friends here. Frank would have to be crazy to come down here and make trouble. In addition to the jail time, he drew a year's probation. They'll check on him. He wouldn't want to risk having to go back to jail to finish his sentence."

"You think so?" she wondered. She recalled what a hardheaded man Frank was. He got even with people. She'd heard things from one of her coworkers in San Antonio at the animal clinic, one who was friends with Frank's sister. She'd said that Frank had run a man off the road who'd reported him for making threats at one of his jobs. The man was badly injured, but he could never prove it had been Frank who'd caused the accident. Cappie was sure, now, that there had probably been other incidents, as well. Frank had admitted to her once that he'd spent time in juvenile hall as a youngster. He'd never said what for.

"He won't be able to get to you at home," Kell continued, "because I keep firearms and I know how to use them," he added grimly. "At work, I don't think he'd dare approach you. Dr. Rydel would likely propel him headfirst out the front door," he chuckled.

Cappie was reminded that Dr. Rydel had actually done that. Dr. King told her about it. A man had come in with a badly injured dog, one with multiple fractures, claiming that the animal had fallen down some steps. After examining the dog, Dr. Rydel knew better. He'd accused the man of abusing the dog, and the man had thrown a punch at him. Dr. Rydel had picked him up and literally thrown him out onto the front porch, while fascinated pet owners watched. Then he'd called the police and had the man arrested. There had been a conviction, too.

Cappie, remembering that, smiled. "Dr. Rydel gets very upset when people abuse animals," she told her brother.

"Obviously." He pursed his lips. "I wonder why he decided to become a veterinarian?"

"I'll have to ask him that."

"Yes, you will. I made macaroni and cheese for supper," he said, "when you called to say you'd be late."

She made a face before she could stop herself.

Kell just grinned. "It's frozen," he said. "I heated it up in the oven."

She sighed with relief. "Sorry. It's just that I've had my carbon for today."

He laughed. "I know I can't cook. One day, though, I'll learn how. Then watch out."

"Some men are born to be chefs. You aren't one of them. I'll make a salad to go with the macaroni."

"I did that already. It's in the fridge."

She went to kiss his cheek, bending over him in the wheelchair. "You're the nicest brother in the whole world."

"I could return the compliment." He ruffled her hair. "Listen, kid, if the surly vet proposes, you take him up on it. I can take care of myself."

"You can't cook," she wailed.

"I can buy nice frozen things to heat up," he returned.

She sighed. "As if Dr. Rydel would ever propose," she laughed. "He likes me, but that doesn't mean he'll want to marry me one day."

"You need to invite him over again and make that shrimp and pasta dish you do so well. I have it from a spy that Dr. Rydel is partial to shrimp."

"Really? Who knows that?"

"Cy Parks told me."

She gave him a suspicious look. "Did you try to pump Cy Parks for inside information?"

Kell gave her his best angelic look. "I would never do such a sneaky thing."

"Sure you would," she retorted.

"Well, Dr. Rydel knew why Cy was asking him, anyway. He just laughed and asked if there was any other inside information that Cy would like to have for us."

She flushed. "Oh, my."

"Cy said the good doctor talked more about you than he did about the heifer he was helping to deliver," Kell added. "It's well-known that Dr. Rydel can't abide women. People get curious when a notorious woman hater suddenly starts seeing a local woman."

"I wonder why he hates women?" she wondered aloud.

"Ask him. But for now, let's eat. I'm fairly empty."

"Goodness, yes, it's two hours past our usual suppertime," she agreed, moving into the kitchen. "I'm sorry I was late."

"How's the dog?" he asked, joining her at the table.

"He'll be fine, Dr. Rydel said. The poor boy was just devastated. I felt sorry for his dad. He'd just lost his job. You could see he was torn between getting the dog treated and taking care of his family. There's a new baby. Dr. Rydel didn't charge him a penny."

"Heart of gold," Kell said gently.

"We were going to take up a collection, when Dr. Rydel reminded us that he drove a Land Rover," she laughed. "He inherited money from his grandmother, Dr. King said, and he makes a good living as a vet."

"That means he'll be able to take care of you when you get married."

She made a face. "Horses before carts, not carts before horses."

"You wait and see," he replied. "That's a man who's totally hooked. He just doesn't know it yet."

She smiled from ear to ear as she started putting food on the table. She'd already pushed her fears about Frank to the back of her mind. Kell was right. He surely wouldn't risk his freedom by making trouble for Cappie again.

Dr. Rydel took her to a carnival Friday night. She was shocked not only at the invitation, but at the choice of outings.

"You like carnivals?" she'd exclaimed.

"Sure! I love the rides and cotton candy." He'd smiled with reminiscence. "My grandmother used to save her egg money to take me to any carnival that came through Jacobsville when I was a kid. She'd even go on the rides with me. I get tickled even now when I hear somebody talk about grandmothers who bake cookies and knit and sit in rocking chairs. My grandmother was a newspaper reporter. She was a real firecracker."

She was remembering the conversation as they walked down the sawdust-covered aisles between booths where carnies were enticing customers to pitch pennies or throw baseballs to win prizes.

"What are you brooding about?" he teased.

She looked up, laughing. "Sorry. I was remembering what you said about your grandmother. Did you spend a lot of time with her?"

His face closed up.

"Sorry," she said again, flushing. "I shouldn't have asked something so personal."

He stopped in the aisle and looked down at her, enjoying the glow of her skin against the pale yellow sweater she was wearing with jeans, her blond hair long and soft around her shoulders.

His big, lean hand went to her hair and toyed with it, sending sweet chills down her spine when he moved a step closer. "She raised me," he said quietly. "My mother and father never got along. They separated two or three times a year, and then fought about who got to keep me. My mother loved me, but my father only wanted me to spite her." His face hardened. "When I made him mad, he took it out on my pets. He shot one of my dogs when I talked back to him. He wouldn't let me take the dog to a veterinarian, and I couldn't save it. That's why I decided to become a vet."

"I did wonder," she confessed. "You talk about your mother, but never about your father. Or your stepfather." Her hands went to his shirtfront. She could feel the warm muscle and hair under the soft cotton.

He sighed. His hand covered one of hers, smoothing over her fingernails. "My stepfather thought that being a vet was a sissy profession, and he said so, frequently. He didn't like animals, either."

"Some sissy profession," she scoffed. "I guess he never had to wrestle down a sick steer that weighed several hundred pounds."

He chuckled. "No, he never did. We got along somewhat. But I don't miss seeing him. I had hard feelings against him for a long time, for letting my mother get so sick that medical science couldn't save her. But sometimes we blame people when it's just fate that bad things happen. Remember the old saying, 'man proposes and God disposes'? It's pretty much true."

"Ah, you advocate being a leaf on the river, grasshopper," she said in a heavily accented tone.

"You lunatic," he laughed, but he bent and kissed her nose. "Yes. I do advocate being a leaf on the river. Sometimes you have to trust that things will work out the way they're meant to, not the way you want them to."

"Why do you hate women?"

His eyebrows arched.

"Everybody knows that you do. You even told me so." She flushed a little as she remembered when he'd told her so; the first time he'd kissed her.

"Remember that, do you?" he teased softly. "You don't know a lot about kissing," he added.

She moved restlessly. "I don't get in much practice."

"Oh, I think I can help you with that," he said in a deep, husky tone. "And for the record, I don't hate you."

"Thank you very much," she said demurely, and peered up at him through her lashes.

He bent slowly to her mouth. "You're very welcome," he whispered. His lips teased just above hers, coaxing her to lift her chin, so that he had better access to her mouth.

Before he could kiss her, a deep voice mused from behind him, "Lewd behavior in public will get you arrested."

"Kilraven," Bentley groaned, turning to face the man. "What are you doing here?"

Kilraven, in full uniform, grinned at the discomfort in their faces as he moved closer and lowered his voice. "I'm investigating possible cotton candy fraud."

"Excuse me?" Cappie said.

"I'm going to taste the cotton candy, and the candy apples, and make sure they're not using illegal counterfeit sugar."

They both stared at him as if he'd gone mad.

He shrugged. "I'm really off duty, I just haven't gone home to change. I like carnivals," he added, laughing. "Jon, my brother, and I used to go to them when we were kids. It brings back happy memories."

"They have a sharpshooting target," Bentley told him.

"I don't waste my unbelievable talent on games," Kilraven scoffed.

"I am in awe of your modesty," Bentley said.

"Why, thank you," Kilraven replied. "I consider it one of my best traits, and I do have quite a few of them." He peered past them. Winnie Sinclair, in jeans and a pretty pink sweater and matching denim jacket, was walking around the penny-pitching booth with her brother, Boone Sinclair, and his wife, Cappie's coworker, Keely. Kilraven looked decidedly uneasy. "I'll see you around," he added.

But instead of going to the cotton candy booth, he turned on his heel and walked right out of the carnival.

"How odd," Cappie murmured, watching him leave.

"Not so odd," Bentley replied. His eyes were on Winnie Sinclair, who'd just seen Kilraven glare in her direction and then walk away. She looked devastated. "Winnie Sinclair is sweet on him," he explained, "and he's even a worse woman hater than I am."

Cappie followed his glance. Keely smiled and waved. She waved back. Winnie Sinclair smiled wanly, and turned back to the booth. "Poor thing," she murmured. "She's so rich, and so unhappy."

"Money doesn't make you happy," Bentley pointed out.

"Well, the lack of it can make you pretty miserable," she said absently.

His hand reached down and locked into hers, bringing her surprised eyes back up to meet his.

She was hesitant, because Keely was grinning in their direction.

"I don't care about public opinion," Bentley pointed out, "and she wouldn't dare tease me in my own practice," he added with a grin.

Cappie laughed. "Okay. I won't care, either."

His strong fingers linked with hers, while he held her gaze. "I can't remember the last time I smiled so much," he said. "I like being with you, Cappie."

She smiled. "I like being with you, too."

They were still smiling at each other when two running children bumped into them and broke the spell.

BENTLEY DROVE HER home, but he didn't move to open the door after he cut off the lights and the engine. He unfastened her seat belt, and his own, and pulled her across the seat and into his lap. Before she could speak, his mouth was hard on hers, grinding into it, and his fingers were lazily searching under the soft hem of her sweater.

She wanted to protest. It was too soon. But he found the hooks on her bra and loosened them with one quick motion of his hand. Then he found soft flesh and teased around it with such expertise that she squirmed backward to give him access.

"Too quick?" he whispered against her mouth.

"No," she bit off, and arched her back.

He smiled as his mouth covered hers once more, and his hand settled directly over the hard little nub that raised against his palm.

After a few minutes, kissing was no longer enough. His hand moved in at the base of her spine and half lifted her against him, so that her belly ground against his in the rapt silence of the vehicle, broken only by the force of their audible breaths, and her soft moan. She could feel him wanting her. It had been exciting with Frank, but not like this. She wanted what Bentley wanted. She was on fire for him.

He unfastened the buttons on his shirt and

pulled her against him, so that her soft breasts ground against the hair-roughened muscles of his chest. His hand moved her hips against his in a slow, anguished rotation that made her moan louder.

"Oh, God," he bit off, shivering. "Cappie!"

Her nails were scoring his back as she held on for dear life and began to shudder. "Don't stop," she whimpered. "Don't stop!"

"I've...got to!"

He moved abruptly, pushing her back into her seat. He opened the door and got out of the Land Rover, standing with his back to her as he sucked in deep breaths and tried to regain the control he'd almost lost.

Embarrassed, Cappie fumbled her bra closures into place and pulled her sweater down. She was still shaky. It had been a near thing. Thank goodness they were parked in her driveway instead of on some lonely road where there might not have been as much incentive to stop. Despite her passionate response to him, Cappie didn't move with the times. Did he know that? Was he hoping for some brief fling? She couldn't. She just couldn't. Now, she reasoned with something like panic, he wouldn't want to see her again, not if she said no. And either way, how was it going to affect her job?

There was only one veterinary clinic in Jacobs County, and she worked for it. If she lost her job, she couldn't get another, not in her field.

While she was torturing herself with such thoughts, the door suddenly opened.

"I know," Bentley said in a strangely calm and amused tone, "you're kicking yourself mentally for taking advantage of me in a weak moment. But it's okay. I'm used to women trying to ravish me."

She stared up at him wide-eyed and speechless. Of all the things she expected he might say, that was the last.

"Come on, come on, you're not going to get a second shot at me in the same night," he teased. "I have my reputation to think of!"

Her mind started working again, and she laughed with relief. She picked up her purse and scrambled out the door, her discarded coat over one arm.

"Listen," he said gently, "don't start brooding. We got a little too involved, too quickly, but we'll deal with it."

She hesitated. "I'm not, well, modern," she blurted out.

"Neither am I, honey," he said softly.

She could have melted into the ground at the husky endearment. She blushed.

He bent and kissed her with tender respect. "I know what sort of woman you are," he said gently. "I'm not going to push you into something you don't want."

"Thanks."

"On the other hand, you have to make me a similar promise," he pointed out. "I'm not going to keep dating you if I have to worry about being ravished every time I bring you home. I'm not that sort of man," he added haughtily.

She grinned from ear to ear. "Okay."

He walked her to the door, smiling complacently. "I'll see you at work Monday," he said. He framed her face in his hands and looked at her for a long time. "Just when you think you're safe," he mused, "you jump headfirst into the tiger trap."

"You know, I was just thinking the same thing," she said facetiously.

He chuckled as he bent to kiss her again. "We'll take it at a nice, easy pace," he whispered. "But I know already how it's going to end up. We're good together. And I'm tired of living alone."

Her heart almost burst with joy. "I...I don't think I could just live with someone," she blurted out, still a little worried.

He kissed her eyes shut. "Neither could I, Cappie," he whispered. "We can talk about licenses and rings." He lifted his head. His eyes were soft with feeling. "But not tonight. We have all the time in the world."

"Yes," she whispered. Her eyes were bright with the force of her emotions. "It's happening so fast."

He nodded. "Like lightning striking."

She felt her heart racing. But in the back of her mind, there was a sudden fear, a foreboding. She bit her lower lip. "You don't really know much about me," she began. "You see, when I lived in San Antonio, there was this man I dated…"

Before she could tell him about Frank, his phone rang. He jerked it out and answered it. "Rydel," he said. He listened, grimaced. "I'll be in the office in ten minutes. Bring the cat right in, I'll see it. Yes. Yes. You're welcome." He hung up. "I have to go."

"Be careful," she said.

He smiled. "I will. Good night."

"Good night, Dr. Rydel."

"Bentley."

She laughed. "Bentley."

He ran back to the Land Rover, started it and drove away with a wave of his hand. Cappie watched him go, then walked into her house, feeling as if she could have floated all the way.

MONDAY MORNING, CAPPIE still felt light-headed and ecstatic. She'd half expected Bentley to phone her

Saturday or Sunday, considering how involved they'd gotten when he brought her home from the carnival on Friday night. But maybe he'd had emergencies. She hoped he hadn't had second thoughts. She was so crazy about him that she couldn't bear to even think about having him reconsider what he'd said. But she knew that wasn't going to happen. They were already so close that she knew it was going to be forever.

So it came as a shock when she walked in the office and Dr. Rydel met her beaming smile with a cold glare that sent chills down her spine.

"You're late, Miss Drake," he said curtly. "Please try to be on time in the future."

She looked as if she'd been hit in the head by a brick. Keely, at the counter, gave her a sympathetic look.

"I'm…I'm sorry, sir," she stammered.

"I need you to help Keely with an X-ray," he said, and turned away abruptly.

"Right away." She put up her coat and purse and rushed to join Keely, who was going in the room where they kept the medical cages. She took a hair band out of her pocket and scrunched her thick hair into a ponytail with it. Inside, she felt numb.

"It's Mrs. Johnson's cat," Keely explained, wary of being overheard by the vet, who was just going into a treatment room. "She stepped on his paw. It's swollen, and Dr. Rydel is afraid it may be broken. Mrs. Johnson is no lightweight," she added with a grin.

"Yes, I know."

"She had to leave him with us while she went to see her heart doctor. She was very upset. She's just getting over a heart attack, and she's worried about her cat!" she said, smiling. Keely opened the cage and Cappie lifted the old cat. It just purred. It didn't even offer to bite her, although it was obvious that it was in pain.

"What a sweet old fellow," Cappie murmured as they went toward the X-ray room. "I thought he might want to bite us."

"He's a sweetheart all right. Here." Keely motioned to the X-ray table and closed the door behind them. "What in the world is wrong with Dr. Rydel?" she whispered. "He came in looking like a thundercloud."

"I don't know," Cappie said. "We went to the carnival Friday night and he was happy and laughing…"

"You didn't have a fight?" Keely persisted.

"No!" She wanted to add that they'd talked

about rings, but this wasn't a good time. The tall man who met her at the door didn't look as if he'd ever said any such thing to her.

"I wonder what happened."

"So do I," Cappie said miserably.

They got the X-ray and Cappie took the old cat back to his cage while Keely developed it. Dr. King gave her a worried look, but she was too busy to say much. Cappie felt sick. She couldn't imagine what had turned Dr. Rydel into an enemy.

She waited and worried all day through two dozen patients and one long emergency. Mrs. Johnson came to pick up her cat, his paw in a neat cast, crying buckets because she'd been so worried about him. Cappie helped her out the door, smiling even though she didn't feel like it. Earlier, she'd thought maybe Dr. Rydel would say something to her, explain, anything. But he didn't. He treated her just as he had when she first joined the practice, courteous but cold.

At the end of the day, she wanted to wait around and see if she could get him to talk to her, but a large animal call took him out the door just minutes before the staff went home. She drove to her house with her heart in her shoes.

"YOU LOOK LIKE the end of the world," Kell remarked when she walked in. "What happened?"

"I don't know," she said sadly. "Dr. Rydel looked at me as if I had some contagious disease and he didn't say one kind word all day. It was business as usual. He was just like he was when I first went to work for him."

"He seemed pleasant enough when he picked you up Friday night," he remarked.

"And when he brought me home," she added. "Maybe he got cold feet."

Kell studied her sad face. "Maybe he did. Everybody says he was the biggest woman hater around town. But if that's the case, he might warm up again when he's had time to think about it. If he's really interested, Cappie, he's not going away."

"You think so?" she asked, hopeful.

"I know so. Men who act like he did when he came to supper don't suddenly turn ice-cold for no reason. Maybe he just had a rough weekend."

Which was no reason for him to take it out on Cappie. On the other hand, she didn't really know him that well.

"Maybe I can get him to talk to me tomorrow," she said.

He smiled. "Maybe you can."

She nodded. "I'll go make supper."

"Try not to worry."

"Of course."

BUT SHE DID worry, and she didn't sleep. She went in to work the next morning with a feeling of foreboding.

Dr. Rydel was at the counter when she came in.

"I'm five minutes early," she said abruptly when he glared at her.

"Come into my office, please," he said.

She brightened. At last, he was going to explain. Surely it was something that didn't have anything to do with her.

He let her in and closed the door behind her. He didn't offer her a seat. He perched on the edge of his desk and stared at her coldly. "I had a visitor Saturday morning."

"You did?" An ex-girlfriend, she was thinking, and he wanted her back, was that it?

"Yes," he replied curtly. "Your boyfriend."

"My what?"

"Your boyfriend, Frank Bartlett," he said coldly.

She felt sick all the way to her toes. Frank had come down here! He'd come to Jacobsville! She held on to a chair. She should have told Bentley about him. She shouldn't have waited. "He's my ex-boyfriend," she began.

He laughed coldly. "Is he, really? Now that's not what he said."

CHAPTER SEVEN

CAPPIE COULD ALMOST imagine what sort of story Frank had told Bentley. But now she understood his anger.

"I can explain," she began.

"You told me Friday night that you had an ex-boyfriend," he said icily. "I didn't get to hear the rest of the story, but Bartlett was kind enough to fill me in. You accused him of assaulting you and had him arrested. He actually spent time in jail and now he has a felony record because of you."

Her eyes widened. "Yes, but that isn't what happened…!"

"I know all about women who like to play with men," he interrupted. "When I was in my early twenties, I worked for a veterinarian while I was in college. It supplemented my grants and scholarships. He had a vet tech who was very pretty, but never got dates. I felt sorry for her. She could only work for him part-time, because I had the full-time position. She stayed late one weekend and teased me into kissing her. Then she very calmly tore her shirt, messed up her hair and phoned the police."

Cappie felt her face go pale.

"She wanted my job," Bentley continued cynically. "I dipped into my savings to hire a private detective, who discovered that it wasn't the first time she'd pulled that stunt. She was arrested and my record was cleared. The vet hired me back in a heartbeat and spent years trying to make it up to me."

"I had no idea," she whispered.

"Of course not, or you wouldn't have tried the same stunt on me."

She blinked in disbelief. "What?"

"You were always talking about what you'd do if you had money. You knew I was well-to-do. When were you going to accuse me of assaulting you? Have you got a lawyer waiting in the wings to sue me?"

She couldn't believe her ears. He actually thought she was playing him for cash. Frank had lied to him, and with his background, Bentley had fallen for the tall tale.

"I've never accused anyone falsely," she defended herself.

"Only Frank Bartlett?"

She swallowed, hard. "He broke my arm," she said with quiet dignity. "It wasn't the first time he hit me, either."

"He told me you'd say that," he replied. "Poor guy. You ruined his life. Well, you aren't going to get the chance to ruin mine. You can work your two weeks' notice." He got to his feet.

"You're firing me?" she asked weakly.

"No, you're quitting," he returned coldly. "That way, you won't be able to let the state support you with unemployment insurance, or sue me for unlawful termination of employment."

"I see."

"Women," he muttered coldly. "You'd think I'd already learned my lesson. You all look so innocent. And you all lie."

He opened the door. "Back to work, Miss Drake," he said in a formal tone. "It's going to be a long day."

She worked mechanically, even managed to smile at old Mr. Smith's jokes and Dr. King's bland comments. Keely was looking at her oddly, but nobody else seemed to find her behavior out of the ordinary.

At the end of the day, she went to her car almost gratefully. She still couldn't believe that Dr. Rydel had fallen for Frank's lies. But she was going to do something about it. She just didn't know what. Yet.

She pulled up in the front yard, puzzled at the colorful cloth piled at the foot of the steps. Was Kell cleaning house…?

She slammed on the brakes, cut off the engine and ran as fast as she could to the front door. That wasn't a bundle of cloth, it was Kell. Kell! He was unconscious, lying beside the wreck of his wheelchair and he was bleeding from half a dozen cuts. She felt for a pulse and, thank God, found one! At least he was still alive.

She saw the front door standing open and didn't dare go inside, for fear someone might be waiting there. She ran back to her car, jerked out her cell phone and punched in 911. Then she ran back to Kell and waited.

THE NEXT HOUR was a blur of ambulance sirens, police sirens, blue uniforms, tan uniforms and abject terror.

She waited for Dr. Micah Steele to come out and tell her what Kell's condition was. She was sick and chilled to the bone. If Kell died, she'd have nobody.

He came back out to the waiting room a few

minutes after Kell was brought in, tall and blond and somber.

"How is he?" she asked frantically.

"Badly beaten," he told her, "which you already know. His back is one long bruise. We're still doing tests, but he has some feeling in his legs, which indicates that the shrapnel in his back may have shifted. If the tests verify that, I'm having him transported to the medical center in San Antonio. I have a friend who's an orthopedic surgeon there. He'll operate."

"You mean, Kell could walk again?" she asked, excited.

He smiled. "Yes." The smile faded. "But that's not my immediate concern. He said there were three men. One of them was a man you've had dealings with, I understand. Frank Bartlett."

"Beating up a paralyzed man, with a mob," she gritted. "What a brave little worm he is!"

"Sheriff's got an all-points bulletin out for him and his friends," Micah told her. "But you're in danger until they're found. You can't stay out there at the house by yourself."

"If you send Kell to San Antonio," she said, "I'll call a friend who works for the same veterinary practice that employed me until I moved here. She'll let me stay with her."

"You'll have to be in protective custody," Micah said firmly.

She smiled. "Her brother is a Texas Ranger. He lives with her."

"Well!"

"I'll call her as soon as I see Kell."

"That will be another twenty minutes," he said. "We have to finish the tests first. But he's going to be fine."

"Okay. Thanks, Dr. Steele."

He smiled. "Glad I can help. I like Kell."

"I do, too."

SHE PHONED BRENDA Banks in San Antonio. Brenda's brother, Colter, was a Texas Ranger. He'd been based out of Houston until his best friend, a Houston police officer named Mike Johns, was killed trying to stop a bank robbery. Colter had asked for reassignment to Company D of the Texas Rangers, based in Bexar County, and moved in with his sister. Since Company D now had an official Cold Case sergeant, Colter applied for and obtained the job. Brenda said he loved solving old cases.

She tried the apartment, first, and sure enough, Brenda was at home and not at work. "How do you like your new job?" Brenda asked when she heard Cappie's voice.

"I like it a lot. Do you still have a spare bed-room, and is there a job opening there at the vet clinic?"

"Oh, dear."

"Yes, well, things didn't work out as well as I hoped," Cappie said quietly. "Frank and a couple of friends came down and almost beat Kell to death. He's on his way up to San Antonio for back sur-gery and I need a place to stay, just until after the surgery. They wanted me in protective custody, but I told them Colter lived with you..."

"You poor kid! You can come and stay as long as you like," Brenda said at once. "But Colter's out of the country on a case. He has an apartment of his own now. What's that about Kell?" she asked worriedly. "Is he going to be all right?"

"He's just banged up, mostly," Cappie said, "but the shrapnel in his back has shifted and he has feeling in his legs. They may be able to operate."

"What a blessing in disguise," the other woman said quietly. "But what about you? Don't tell me Frank went to your house just to beat up your brother."

"He was probably looking for me," she con-fessed. "But he'd already done enough damage to my working relationship with my new boss. I don't have a job anymore, either."

"I'll ask Dr. Lammers about something part-time," she said immediately. "I know they'd love to have you back. The new tech doesn't have the dedication to the job that you had, and doesn't show up for work half the time, either. I'll phone her right now. Meanwhile, you come on up here. You know where the spare key's kept."

"Thanks a million, Brenda." Her voice was breaking, despite her efforts to control it.

"Honey, I'm so sorry," Brenda said gently. "If there's anything I can do, anything at all, you just tell me."

Cappie swallowed. "I've missed you."

"I've missed you, too. You just hang on. Get Kell up here and then come on yourself. We'll handle it. Okay?"

"Okay."

"I'll phone Dr. Lammers right now." She hung up.

Cappie went back to the waiting room and sat, sad and somber, while she waited for the test results and a chance to talk to Kell.

Dr. Steele was smiling when he came back. "I think it's operable," he said. "I'm going to send Kell to San Antonio by chopper. It's quicker and it will be easier on his back. We don't want that shrapnel to shift again. You can see him, just for a minute. Want to fly up with him?"

"Yes, if I can," she said.

He nodded toward Kell's room. "Cash Grier is in there with him. He wants a word with you, too."

"Okay. Thanks, Dr. Steele."

She opened the door and walked in. Cash Grier was leaning against the windowsill, very somber. Kell looked terrible, but he smiled when she bent over to kiss him.

"Dr. Steele thinks they may be able to operate," she told him.

"So I heard." He smiled. "I don't know how I'll afford it, but maybe they take IOUs."

"You get better before you worry about money," she said firmly. "We can always sell the car."

"Sure, that will pay for my aspirin," Kell chuckled.

"Stop that. It's going to work out," she said firmly. "Hi, Chief," she greeted Cash.

"Hi, yourself. Your ex-boyfriend was after you," he said without preamble. "He won't quit. He knows he'll go back to jail for what he did to Kell. He'll get you, if he can, before we catch him."

"I'm going to fly up to San Antonio with Kell," she said slowly, "and I'll be staying with my best friend. Her brother's a Texas Ranger." She didn't add that he was out of town. After all, Cash wouldn't know. But would she be putting Brenda in danger, just by being there?

"Colter's out of the country, and Brenda doesn't own a weapon," Cash said, stone-faced. He nodded when she gasped. "I know Colter. I used to be a Texas Ranger, too. We've kept in touch. You don't want to put Brenda in the line of fire."

"I was just worrying about that." She bit her lower lip. "Then what do we do?"

"You stay in a hotel near the hospital," he said. "We're sending security up to watch you."

"Police officers from here?" she wondered.

"Not really," Cash said slowly. "Actually Eb Scott is detailing two of his men to stay with you. One is just back from the Middle East, and the other is waiting for an assignment."

"Mercenaries," she said softly.

"Exactly."

She looked worried.

"They're not the sort you see in movies," Kell assured her. "These guys have morals and they only work for good causes, not just for money."

"Do you know the men?" she asked him.

He hesitated.

"I know them," Cash said at once. "And you can

trust them. They'll take care of you. Just go with Kell to the hospital and they'll meet you there."

She frowned. "I'll have to phone somebody at my office, to tell them what's happened."

"Everybody at your office already knows what happened," Cash told her. "Well, except your boss," he added, just when her heart had skipped two beats. "He had to fly to Denver on some sort of personal business. Something to do with his stepfather."

"Oh." It was just as well, she thought. Now she wouldn't have to see him again. Kell didn't know Dr. Rydel had fired her, but this wasn't really the time to tell him. It could wait. "What about our house?"

"Kell gave me the key," he said. "I'll get it to Keely. She'll make sure the lights are off and everything's locked up and the fridge is cleaned out."

"I don't want to live there anymore," she told Kell in a subdued tone.

"We don't have to make decisions right now," he replied, wincing as he moved. "Hell, I think it was better when I couldn't feel my legs!"

"You'll enjoy walking again," Cappie said gently. "Kell, it would be like a miracle. At least some good would have come out of all this."

"Just what I was thinking." He smiled at her. "Now don't worry. It's going to work out."

"Yes, it is," Cash agreed. "Rick Marquez is going to make sure every cop in San Antonio has a personal description of Frank Bartlett, and he's talked to a reporter he knows at one of the news stations. Your nemesis Frank is going to be so famous that if he walks into a convenience store, ten people are going to tackle him and yell for the police."

"Really? But why?"

"Did I mention that there's a reward for his capture?" Cash added. "We took up a little collection."

"How kind!"

"You should stay here," Cash said seriously. "It's a good town. Good people."

Her face closed up. "I'm not living in any town that also houses Dr. Rydel."

Cash and Kell exchanged a long look.

"But Kell might like to stay," she added.

Kell wondered what was going on. Cappie had been crazy about her boss until today. "I think we need to have a talk about why you're down on your boss," he told her.

"Tomorrow," she said. "First thing."

"I'll probably be in surgery tomorrow, first thing," Kell replied.

She smiled wanly. "Then I'll tell you while you're unconscious. When do we leave?" she added.

Kell wanted to argue, but they'd given him something for pain, and he was already drooping. "As soon as the helicopter gets here. Need anything from the house? I'm sure Cash would run you over there."

She shook her head. "I've got my purse and my phone. Oh, here's the house key," she added, pulling it off her key ring and handing it to Cash. "I know you gave Kell's to Keely, but you may need mine. Thanks a lot."

"If you need anything, you can call Keely. She'll run it up to you, or her husband or her sister-in-law will."

"I'll do that."

"And try not to worry," Cash added, moving away from the window. "Things always seem darkest before the dawn. Believe me, I should know," he added with a smile. "I've seen my share of darkness."

"You're a wonderful police chief," she told him.

"Another good reason to stay in Jacobs County," he advised.

"We can agree to disagree on that point," she

replied. "I might reconsider if you'd lock Dr. Rydel up and throw away the key."

"Can't do that. He's the best veterinarian around."

"I guess he is, at that."

Cash wisely didn't add to his former statement.

THE TRIP IN the helicopter was fascinating to Cappie, who'd never flown in one, despite Kell's years in the military. She'd had the opportunity, but she was afraid of the machines. Now, knowing that it was helping to save Kell's legs, she changed her opinion of them.

She sat quietly in her seat, smiling at the med techs, but not talking to them. She'd had just about all she could stand of men, she decided, for at least the next twenty years. She only hoped and prayed that Kell would be able to walk again. And that somebody would find Frank Bartlett before he came back to finish what he'd started.

BENTLEY RYDEL WALKED into his office three days later, out of sorts and even more irritable than he'd been when he left. His stepfather had suffered a stroke. It hadn't killed him, but he was temporarily paralyzed on one side and in a nursing home for the foreseeable future. Bentley had tracked down the man's younger brother and made arrangements to fly him to Denver to look after his sibling. All that had taken time. He didn't begrudge giving help, but he was still upset about Cappie. Why had he been stupid enough to get involved with her? Hadn't he learned his lesson about women by now?

The office hadn't officially opened for business; it was ten minutes until it did. He found every employee in the place standing behind the counter glaring at him as if he'd invented disease.

His eyebrows arched. "What's going on?" His face tautened. "Cappie's suing me for asking her to quit, is she?" he asked with cold sarcasm.

Dr. King glared back. "Cappie's in San Antonio with her brother," she said. "Her ex-boyfriend and two of his friends beat Kell within an inch of his life."

He felt the blood drain out of his face. "What?"

"They've got Cappie surrounded by police and volunteers, trying to keep the same thing from happening to her," Keely added curtly. "Sheriff Carson checked into Frank Bartlett's background and found several priors for battery against women, but nobody was willing to press charges until Cappie did. She wasn't exactly willing at that—her brother forced her to, when she got out of the hospital. Bartlett beat her bloody and broke her arm.

She said that she'd probably be dead if Kell hadn't managed to knock out Bartlett in time."

He felt as if his throat had been cut. He'd believed the man. How could he have done that to Cappie? How could he have suspected her of such deceit? She'd been the victim. Bentley had believed the lying ex-boyfriend and fired Cappie. Now she was in danger and it was his fault.

"Where is she?" he asked heavily.

"She told us not to tell you," Dr. King said quietly. "She doesn't want to see you again. In fact, she's got her old job back in San Antonio and she's going to live there."

He felt sick all over. No, she wouldn't want to stay in Jacobs County now. Not after the job Bentley had done on her self-esteem. It had probably been hard for her to trust a man again, having been physically assaulted. She'd trusted Bentley. She'd been kind and sweet and trusting. And he'd kicked her in the teeth.

He didn't answer Dr. King. He looked at his watch. "Get to work, people," he said in a subdued tone.

Nobody answered him. They went to work. He went into his office, closed the door and picked up the telephone.

"Yes?" Cy Parks answered.

"Where's Cappie?" he asked quietly.

"If I tell you, I'll have to change my name and move to a foreign country," Cy replied dryly.

"Tell me anyway. I'll buy you a fake mustache."

Cy chuckled. "Okay. But you can't tell her I sold her out."

"Fair enough."

CAPPIE WAS WORN-OUT. She'd been in the waiting room around the clock until Kell was through surgery, and it had taken a long time. The chairs must have been selected for their comfort level, she decided, to make sure nobody wanted to stay in them longer than a few minutes. It was impossible to sleep in one, or even to doze. Her back was killing her. She needed sleep, but she couldn't leave the hospital until she knew Kell was out of the recovery room.

Beside her, two tall, somber men sat waiting also. One of them was dark-eyed and dark-headed, and he never seemed to smile. The other one had long blond hair in a ponytail and one pale brown eye and an eye-patch on the other. He was good-natured about his disability and referred to himself as Dead-Eye. He chuckled as he said it. She didn't know their names.

Detective Sergeant Rick Marquez had dropped

by earlier in the day to talk to her about Frank Bartlett's family and friends. She did know about Frank's sister, but she hadn't met any of his friends. Detective Marquez was, she thought, really good-looking. She wondered why he didn't have a steady girlfriend.

Marquez had assured her that he was doing everything possible to track down Frank Bartlett, and that a friend of his who was a news anchor was going to broadcast a description of Bartlett and ask for help from the public to apprehend him. There was a two-thousand-dollar reward being offered for information leading to his arrest and conviction.

Brenda came with her to the hospital and stayed until she was called into her own office for an emergency surgery on a dog patient. She'd promised to return as soon as she could. She was upset that Cappie wasn't going to stay with her. She could borrow a gun, she muttered, and shoot that two-legged snake if he came near the apartment. But Cappie smiled and said she hadn't been thinking straight when she'd called and asked for a place to stay. She wasn't risking Brenda. Besides, she had security. Brenda gave the two men a long, curious glance. She did mention that she wouldn't want to mess with them, if she was a bad man. The one with the ponytail grinned at her.

After Brenda left, Cappie sat with her two somber male attachments while people came and went in the waiting room. She drank endless cups of black coffee and tried not to dwell on her fears. If Kell could just walk again, she told herself, the misery of the past few days would be worth it. If only!

Finally the surgeon on Kell's case came out to speak with her, smiling in his surgical greens.

"We removed the shrapnel," he told her. "I'm confident that we got it all. Now we wait for results, once your brother has time to heal. But I'm cautiously optimistic that he'll walk again."

"Oh, thank God," she breathed, giving way to tears. "Thank God!"

"Now, will you please go and get some sleep?" he asked. "You look like death walking."

"I'll do that. Thank you, Dr. Sims. Thank you so much!"

"You're very welcome. Leave your cell phone number at the nurses' desk and they'll phone you if they need you."

"I'll do that right now."

She went to the nurses' desk with her two companions flanking her and looking all around them covertly.

"I'm Kell Drake's sister," she told a nurse. "I want to give you my cell phone number in case you need to get in touch with me."

"Certainly," a little brunette replied, smiling. She pulled a pad over to her and held a pen poised over it. "Go ahead."

Cappie gave the number to her. "I'll always have it with me, and I won't turn it off."

The brunette looked from one man to the other curiously.

"They're with me," Cappie told her. She leaned over the counter. "You see, they're in terrible danger and I have to protect them."

The two men gave her a simultaneous glare that could have stopped traffic. The brunette managed to smother a giggle.

"Okay, guys, I'm ready whenever you are," she told them.

The one with the eye-patch pursed his lips. "Want a head start?" he asked pointedly.

She grinned up at him. "You want one?" she countered.

He chuckled, and indicated that she could go first. He turned and winked at the little brunette, who flushed with pleasure. He was whistling as he followed Cappie out through the waiting room.

"You, protect us," the other man scoffed. "From what…bug bites?"

"Keep that up," Cappie told him, "and I'll show you a bite."

"Now, now, let's try to get along," Dead-Eye murmured as they waited for the elevator to come back up.

"I'm getting along. She's the one with the attitude problem," the other man muttered.

"Says you," Cappie told him.

He stared at Dead-Eye and pointed at Cappie.

"I never take sides in family squabbles," Dead-Eye told him.

"She is not a member of my family!" the other man said.

"A likely story," Dead-Eye said. "Anyway, how can you be sure? Have you had your DNA compared to hers?"

"I know I'm not related to you," the man told Dead-Eye.

"How do you know that?" came the dry retort.

"Because you're too ugly to be any kin to me."

"Well, I never," Dead-Eye harrumphed. "Look who's calling who *ugly*."

"Your mother dresses you funny, too."

Cappie was already light-headed with relief. These two were setting off her quirky sense of humor. "I can't take the two of you anywhere," she complained. "You embarrass me to tears."

"Can I help it if he's ugly?" the second man said. "I was only stating a fact."

"He's not ugly," Cappie defended Dead-Eye. "He's just unique."

Dead-Eye grinned at her. "We can get married first thing in the morning," he said. "I've been keeping a wedding ring in my chest of drawers for just such an emergency."

Cappie shook her head. "Sorry. I can't marry you tomorrow."

"Why not?"

"My brother won't let me date ugly men."

"You just said I wasn't ugly!" he protested.

"I lied."

"I can have my nose fixed."

She frowned. It was a very nice nose.

"I can alter it for you with my fist," the other man volunteered.

"I can alter you first," Dead-Eye informed him.

"No fighting," Cappie protested. "We'll all end up in jail."

"Some of us have probably escaped from one

recently," the other man said with a pointed look at Dead-Eye.

"I didn't have to escape. They let me out on account of my extreme good looks," Dead-Eye scoffed.

"Your looks are extreme," came the reply. "Just not good."

"If you two don't stop arguing, I'm going to have my best friend come over to spend the night with us, and you two will be sharing the sofa," she assured them.

"Just shoot me now," Dead-Eye muttered, "and be done with it. I'm not sharing anything with him. Not unless he's got proof he isn't rabid."

The elevator door had opened while they were arguing. Dr. Bentley Rydel stepped off it and stared at the younger man while Cappie gaped at his sudden appearance.

"He isn't rabid," Bentley assured Dead-Eye.

"And how would you know?" Dead-Eye asked.

"I'm a veterinarian," Bentley replied curtly.

"We should go," Cappie said, avoiding Bentley's eyes.

"We?" he asked, scowling.

"These are my two new boyfriends," Cappie told him with a cold scowl. "We're sharing a room."

He knew she wasn't involved with two strangers. He had a pretty good idea of who they were and why she was with them. She probably expected him to believe the bald statement, with his track record.

"I heard about Kell," he said quietly. "How is he?"

"Out of surgery and resting comfortably, thank you," she said formally. "We have to go."

"Can we talk?" Bentley asked somberly.

"If you can get them," she indicated her companions, "to tie me up and gag me, sure. Let's go, guys."

She walked into the elevator and stood with her back to the door until she heard it close.

CHAPTER EIGHT

CAPPIE DIDN'T SLEEP, of course. She was replaying the last forty-eight hours in her mind all night, sick with worry about Kell. It was her fault that Frank Bartlett had ever gotten near them. If only she hadn't been so flattered by his attention, so crazy about him that she ignored Kell's warnings. If only she hadn't gone out with him at all.

Pity, she thought, that people couldn't set the clock backward and erase all the stupid things they did. Like getting involved with Dr. Bentley Rydel, for example, she told herself. It had surprised her to find him at the hospital. Somebody in Jacobsville must have told him what had happened, and he felt sorry for her. Maybe he was willing to overlook her smarmy past long enough to check on her brother's condition. That didn't mean he believed her innocence or wanted to get involved with her again. Which was just as well, she told herself, because she certainly wanted nothing more to do with him!

She got up and dressed…in the same clothes she'd worn the day before. She hadn't packed anything. She'd have to call Keely and ask her to go to the house and pack a few items of clothing for her and Kell. But she'd make sure Keely got an armed person to go with her, in case Frank was waiting around to see if Cappie turned back up.

When she opened her bedroom door, the two men were arguing over the coffee in the tiny little coffeepot that came, with coffee, as a perk for staying in the hotel.

"There's not enough for three people," Dead-Eye was muttering, refusing to let go of the pot.

"Then you can get yours at a café, because I'm having mine here," the other man said coldly.

"We're all having ours at the hospital, because I'm leaving right now," Cappie informed them, starting for the door.

"See what you get for starting a fight? Now neither of us is having coffee," Dead-Eye scoffed as he turned off the coffeepot and put the little carafe back in it.

"You started it first," the other man said coolly.

Cappie ignored the banter and opened the door.

"Hold it right there."

Dead-Eye was in front of her in a heartbeat, his hand under his jacket as a tall man walked into view in the hall. He stood immobile, waiting.

But it wasn't Frank. It was another man, and a woman and child suddenly appeared behind him and started talking to him.

"Nice day," Dead-Eye told them with a smile.

"Huh? Oh. Yeah." The man smiled back and herded his family ahead of him down the hall.

Dead-Eye stood aside to let Cappie out. "Wait until one of us makes sure it's safe," he told her in a kind tone. "Men who commit battery without fear of arrest are usually not planning to go back in prison, if you get my drift. He might decide a bullet is better than a fist."

"Sorry," she said. "I didn't think."

"That's what we're here for," the other man said, following her out the door and closing it. "We'll think for you."

"Were you thinking, just then?" Dead-Eye grinned.

The other man indicated his sleeve. The hilt of a large knife was in his palm. He flexed his hand and snapped it back in place. "Learned that from Cy Parks," he said. "He taught me everything I know."

"Then what are you doing with Eb?"

"Learning…diplomacy." He said it through gritted teeth. "They say my attitude needs work."

Dead-Eye opened his mouth to speak.

Cappie beat him to it. "And you think I need an attitude adjustment?" she exclaimed.

The other man shifted restlessly. "We should get to the hospital."

Cappie just smiled. So did Dead-Eye.

WHEN THEY GOT to the hospital cafeteria, it was already full. One of the tables was occupied by a somber Dr. Rydel, moving eggs around on a plate as if he couldn't decide between eating them or throwing them.

Cappie's traitorous heart jumped at the sight of him, but she didn't let her pleasure show. She was still fuming about his assumption of her guilt, without any proof except the word of a man who was a stranger.

He looked up and saw her and grimaced.

"Want me to frisk him for you?" Dead-Eye asked pleasantly. "I can do it discreetly."

"Yeah, like you discreetly frisked that guy at the airport," the dark-eyed man muttered. "Isn't he suing?"

"I apologized," Dead-Eye retorted.

"Before or after airport security showed up?"

"Well, after, but he said he understood how I might have mistaken him for an international terrorist."

"He was wearing a Hawaiian shirt and flip-flops!"

"The best disguise on earth for a spy, and I ought to know. I used to live in Fiji."

"Did you, really?" Cappie asked, fascinated. "I've always wanted to go there."

"Have you?" Dead-Eye looked past her to Bentley, who had gotten up from the table and was moving toward them. "Now might not be a bad time," he advised.

Bentley had dark circles under his eyes from lack of sleep. But he was just as arrogant as ever. He stopped in front of Cappie.

"I'd like to talk to you for a minute."

She didn't want to talk to him, and almost repeated her words of the night before. But she was tired and worried and a little afraid of Frank. It didn't matter now, anyway. Her life in Jacobsville was already over. She and Kell would start over again, here in San Antonio, once the threat was over.

"All right," she said wearily. "I'll only be a minute, guys," she told Dead-Eye and his partner. "You can get coffee."

"Finally," Dead-Eye groaned. "I'm having caffeine withdrawal."

"Is that why you look so ugly?" the other man taunted.

They moved off, still fencing verbally.

"Who are they?" Bentley asked as he seated her at his table.

"Bodyguards," she said. "Eb Scott loaned them to me."

"Want coffee?"

"Please."

He went to the counter, got coffee and a sweet roll and put them in front of her. "You have to eat," he said when she started to argue. "I know you like those. You bring them to work in the morning sometimes when you have to eat on the run."

She shrugged. "Thanks."

He pushed sugar and cream to her side of the table.

"I phoned the nurses' desk on the way here, on my cell phone," she said wearily. "They said Kell's having his bath and then breakfast, so I'd have time to eat before I went up to see him."

"I talked to him briefly last night," he said.

She lifted her eyebrows. "It's family only. They posted it on the door!"

"Oh, that. I told them I was his brother-in-law."

She glared at him over her coffee as she added cream.

"Well, they let me in," he said.

She lifted the cup and sipped the hot coffee, with an expression of absolute delight on her face.

"He was about as friendly as you are," he sighed. "I screwed up."

She nodded. "With a vengeance," she added, still glaring.

He pushed his plate of cold scrambled eggs to one side. His pale blue eyes were intent on her gray ones. "After what happened to me, I was down on women for a long time. When I finally got to the stage where I thought I might be able to trust one again, I found out that she was a lot more interested in what I could give her than what I was." His face tautened. "You get gun-shy, after a while. And I didn't know you, Cappie. We had supper a few times, and I took you to a carnival, but that didn't mean we were close."

She stared at the roll and took a bite of it. It was delicious. She chewed and swallowed and sipped coffee, all without answering. She'd thought they were getting to be close. How dumb could she be?

He drew in a long breath and sipped his own coffee. "Maybe we were getting close," he admitted. "But trust comes hard to me."

She put down the cup and met his eyes evenly. "How hard do you think it comes to me?" she asked baldly. "Frank beat me up. He broke my arm. I spent three days in the hospital. Then at the trial, his defense attorney tried his best to make it look as if I deliberately provoked poor Frank by refusing to go to bed with him! Apparently that was enough to justify the assault, in his mind."

He scowled. "You didn't sleep with him?"

The glare took on sparks. "No. I think people should get married first."

He looked stunned.

She flushed and averted her eyes. "So I live in the past," she muttered. "Kell and I had deeply religious parents. I don't think he took any of it to heart, but I did."

"You don't have to justify yourself to me," he said quietly. "My mother was like you."

"I'm not trying to justify myself. I'm saying that I have an idealistic attitude toward marriage. Frank thought I owed him sex for a nice meal and got furious when I wouldn't cooperate. And for the record, I didn't even really provoke him. He beat me up because I suggested that he needed to drink a little less beer. That was all it took. Kell barely got to me in time."

He let out a long breath. "My stepfather hit my

mother once, for burning the bacon, when they were first married. I was fifteen."

"What did she do?" she asked.

"She told me. I took him out back and knocked him around the yard for five minutes, and told him if he did it again, I'd load my shotgun and we'd have another, shorter, conversation. He never touched her again. He also stopped drinking."

"I don't think that would have worked with Frank."

"I rather doubt it." He studied her wan, drawn face. "You've been through hell, and I haven't helped. For what it's worth, I'm sorry. I know that won't erase what I said. But maybe it will help a little."

"Thanks." She finished her roll and coffee. But when she got through, she put two dollar bills on the table and pushed them toward him.

"No!" he exclaimed, his high cheekbones flushing as he recalled with painful clarity his opinion of her as a gold digger.

"I pay my own way, despite what you think of me," she said with quiet pride. She stood up. "Money doesn't mean so much to me. I'm happy if I can pay bills. I'm sorry I gave you the impression that I'd do anything for it. I won't."

She turned and left him sitting there, with his own harsh words echoing in his mind.

KELL WAS LYING on his stomach in bed. His bruises were much more obvious now, and he was pale and weak from the surgery. She sat down beside him in a chair and smiled.

"How's it going?" she asked gently.

"Badly," he said with a long sigh. "Hurts like hell. But they think I might be able to walk again. They have to wait until I start healing and the bruising abates before they'll know for sure. But I can wiggle my toes." He smiled. "I'm not going to prove it, because it hurts. You can take my word for it."

"Deal." She brushed back his unkempt hair.

"Your old boss came by last night," he said coldly. "He explained what happened. I gave him an earful."

"So did I. He's back."

"I'm not surprised. He was pretty contrite."

"It won't do any good," she said sadly. "I won't forget what he said to me. He didn't believe me."

"Apparently he's had some hard knocks of his own."

"Yes, that explains it, but it doesn't excuse it."

"Point taken." He glanced past her toward the door. "You've got bodyguards."

"Yes. Some of Eb Scott's guys. They don't like each other."

"Chet has a chip on his shoulder, and Rourke likes to take potshots at it."

"Which is which?" she asked.

"Rourke lost an eye overseas."

"Oh. Dead-Eye."

He chuckled and then winced. "That's what he calls himself. He's got quite a history. He worked for the CIA over in the South Pacific for several years. Now he's trying to get back in. His language skills are rusty, and he's not up on the latest communications protocols, so he's studying with Eb. Chet, on the other hand, is trying to land a job doing private security for overseas embassies. He has anger issues."

"Anger issues?"

"He tends to slug people who make him angry. Doesn't go over well in embassies."

"I can understand that." She frowned. "How do you know them?"

He sighed. "That's a long story. We'll have to talk about it when I get out of here."

She was adding up things and getting uncomfortable totals. "Kell, you weren't working for a magazine when you went to Africa, were you?" she asked.

He hesitated. "That's one of the things we'll talk about. But not now. Okay?"

She relented. He did look very rocky. "Okay." She laid a gentle hand on his muscular arm. "You're my brother and I love you. That won't change, even if you tell me blatant lies and think I'll never know about them."

"You're too sharp for your own good."

"I've been told that."

"Don't stray from your bodyguards," he cautioned. "I have to agree with them. I think Frank's not planning to go back to jail. He'll do whatever it takes to get even with you, and then he'll try suicide-by-cop."

"Jail would be better than dead, certainly?"

"Frank has anger issues, too."

She flexed the arm he'd broken. "I noticed."

"Don't take chances. Promise me."

"I promise. Please get well. Being an orphan is bad enough. I can't lose you, too."

He smiled. "I'm not going anywhere. After all, I've got a book to finish. I have to get well in order to do that."

She hesitated. "Kell, he wouldn't come here,

and try to finish the job he did on you?" she asked worriedly.

"I have company."

"You do?"

"Move it, you military rejects," came a deep voice from the door. A tall, familiar-looking man with silver eyes and jet-black hair moved into the room, dressed in boots and jeans and a chambray shirt, carrying a foam cup of coffee.

"Kilraven?" she asked, surprised. "Aren't you working?"

He shook his head. "Not tonight," he said. "I had a couple of vacation days I was owed, so I'm babysitting your brother."

"Thanks," she said with a broad grin.

"I'm getting something out of it," he chuckled. "I'm stuck on the middle level of a video game, and Kell knows how to crack it."

"Is it 'Halo: ODST'?" Dead-Eye asked. "I beat it."

"Yeah, on the 'easy' level, I'll bet," Chet chided.

"I did it on 'normal,' for your information," he huffed.

"Well, I did it on Legendary," Kell murmured, "so shut up and take care of my sister, or I'll wipe the floor with you when I get back on my feet."

Dead-Eye gave him a neat salute. Chet shrugged.

"See you later," Cappie said, kissing her brother's cheek again.

"Where are you going?" he asked.

"On a job interview," she said gently. "Brenda's boss might have something part-time."

"Are you sure you want to move back here?" Kell asked.

"Yes," she lied.

"Good luck, then."

"Thanks. See you, Kilraven. Thank you, too."

He grinned. "Keep your gunpowder dry."

"Tell them." She pointed to her two companions. "I hate guns."

"Bite your tongue!" Kilraven said in mock horror.

She made a face and went out the door, her two companions right behind her.

BENTLEY MET THEM at the elevator. "Where are you going now?" he asked her.

She hesitated.

"Job interview," Rourke said for her.

"You can't leave the clinic," Bentley said curtly. "I don't have anybody to replace you yet!"

"That's your problem," she shot back. "I don't want to work for you anymore!"

He looked hunted.

"Besides, Kell and I are moving back to San Antonio as soon as he heals," she said stubbornly. "It's too far to commute."

Bentley looked even more worried. He didn't say anything.

"Aren't you supposed to be at work?" she added.

"Dr. King's filling in for me," he said.

"Until when?"

His pale eyes glittered. "Until I can convince you to come home where you belong."

"Please. Hold your breath." She walked around him and into the next open elevator. She didn't even look to see which direction it was going.

IT WAS GOING up. She was stuck between two over-size men and two perfume-soaked women. She started to cough before the women got off. The men left two floors later and the elevator slowly started down.

"Wasn't that heaven?" Rourke said with a dreamy smile, inhaling the air. "I love perfume."

"It makes me sick," Chet muttered, sniffing.

"It makes me cough," Cappie agreed.

"Well, obviously, you two don't like women as much as I do," Rourke scoffed.

They both glared at him.

He raised both hands, palms-out, in defense and grinned.

The elevator stopped at the cafeteria again and Bentley was still there, smoldering.

Cappie glared at him. It didn't help. He got on the elevator and pressed the down button.

"Where do you think you're going?" Cappie asked him.

"On a job interview," he said gruffly. "Maybe they need an extra veterinarian where you're applying."

"Does this mean that you're not marrying me?" Rourke wailed in mock misery.

Bentley gaped. "You're marrying him?" he exclaimed.

"I am not marrying anybody!" Cappie muttered.

Bentley shifted restlessly. "You could marry me," he said without looking at her. "I'm established in a profession and I don't carry a gun," he added, looking pointedly at the butt of Rourke's big .45 auto nestled under his armpit.

"So am I, established in a profession," Rourke argued. "And knowing how to use a gun isn't a bad thing."

"Diplomats don't think so," Chet muttered.

"That's only until other people start shooting at them, and you save their butts," Rourke told him.

Chet brightened. "I hadn't thought of it like that."

"Come on," Cappie groaned when the elevator stopped. "I swear, I feel like I'm leading a parade!"

"Anybody got a trombone?" Rourke asked the people waiting around the elevator.

Cappie caught his arm and dragged him along with her.

THEY TOOK A cab to the veterinarian's office. The car was full. The men were having a conversation about video games, but they left Cappie behind when they mentioned innovations they'd found on the Internet, about how to do impossible things with the equipment in the Halo series.

"Using grenades to blow a Scorpion up onto a mountain?" she exclaimed.

"Hey, whatever works," Rourke argued.

"Yeah, but you have to shoot your buddies to get enough grenades," Chet said. "That's not ethical."

"This, from a guy who lifted a policeman's riot gun right out of the trunk of his car!" Rourke said.

"I never lifted it, I borrowed it! Anyway, everybody was shooting rifles or shotguns and I only had a .45," he scoffed.

"Everybody else's was bigger than his," Rourke translated with an angelic pose.

Chet hit his arm. "Stop that!"

"See why he can't get a job with diplomats?" Rourke quipped, holding his arm in mock pain.

"I'm amazed that either of you can get a job," Cappie commented. "You really need to work on your social skills."

"I'm trying to, but you won't marry me," Rourke grumbled.

"Of course she won't, she's marrying me," Bentley said smugly.

"I am not!" Cappie exclaimed.

"No woman is going to marry a veterinarian when she can have a dashing spy," Rourke commented.

"Do you know one?" Bentley asked calmly.

Rourke glared at him. "I can be dashing when I want to, and I used to work for the CIA."

"Yes, but does sweeping floors count as a real job?" Chet wanted to know.

"You ought to know," Rourke told the other man. "Isn't that what you did in Manila?"

"I was the president's bodyguard!"

"And didn't he end up in the hospital?"

"We're here!" Cappie said loudly, indicating where the cab was stopping. "And the ride is Dutch treat," she added. "I'm not paying cab fare for bodyguards and stubborn hangers-on."

"Who's a hanger-on?" Rourke asked.

But Cappie was already out of the cab. The three men followed her when they settled their part of the fare.

She walked into the veterinarian's front office, where Kate Snow was still holding down the job of receptionist. She was twenty-four, tall, brunette and had soft green eyes and a pleasant rather than pretty face. She smiled.

"Hi, Cappie," she greeted. "Come to visit your old stomping grounds?"

"Actually I'm here to apply for something part-time," she replied.

"Brenda said that, but I didn't believe her," Kate replied, stunned. "You just moved to Jacobsville."

"Well, I'm moving back."

"I'll buzz Dr. Lammers," she said, and pressed a button on the phone. She spoke into the receiver, nodded, spoke again and hung up. "He's with a patient, but he'll be out in a minute." She looked past Cappie. "Can I help you?" she asked the three men.

"I'm with her," Rourke said.

"Me, too," Chet seconded.

"I'm applying for a job, too," Bentley said. "I thought you might need an extra vet." He smiled.

"Who are you?" Kate asked, surprised.

"He's my ex-boss," Cappie muttered.

"You're Dr. Rydel?" Kate exclaimed. "But you have your own practice in Jacobsville!"

"I do, but if Cappie moves here, I move here," he said stubbornly.

"We might move here, too," Rourke interrupted. "I can interview for a job here, too. I can type."

"Liar," Chet said. "He can't type."

"I can learn!"

"All you know how to do is shoot people," Chet scoffed.

"Sir, it's illegal to carry a concealed weapon," Kate began nervously.

Rourke gave her his most charming smile. "I'm a professional bodyguard, and I have a permit. If you'd like to see it, I'll take you to this lovely little French bistro downtown and you can look at it while we eat."

Kate stared at him as if he'd grown horns.

"There's a guy stalking her," Chet told her. "We're going to catch him if he tries anything and turn him over to local law enforcement."

"Stalking you?" Kate stammered.

Cappie glared at the two men. "Thank you so much for making me an employment liability!"

Rourke made her a bow. Chet just glowered. Bentley beamed.

"I don't mind employing you. Not one bit," Bentley said. "These two can work for the groomer and we'll protect you."

"I'm not grooming anything," Chet told him bluntly.

"Okay. Then you can deal with surly clients," Bentley compromised.

Chet gave him an appreciative look.

"Actually I know how to groom things," Rourke said. "I once shaved a monkey."

Cappie hit him.

"There you are!" Brenda exclaimed, coming out of the back in a green-and-blue polka-dotted lab coat. "I talked to Dr. Lammers, but he said we've already got more part-timers than we can spare. I'm so sorry," she added miserably.

"What's your address?" Bentley asked. "I'll send you flowers."

"I thought you wanted to marry her," Chet pointed at Cappie.

Brenda's eyes widened. "Who are you?" she asked the dark-eyed man.

"I'm a hired…"

"…assassin," Rourke finished for him.

"I don't kill people, I just shoot them!" Chet growled.

"I only wound them," Rourke added. "Are we going back to Jacobsville, then?"

"Who are these men?" Brenda asked again.

"Well, these two are my bodyguards—" she indicated them "—and that's my ex-boss."

"Why is your ex-boss here?" she asked, all at sea.

"He was going to get a job here, too, but there are no openings for part-timers or vets, so I guess we're all going back to Jacobsville," Cappie said miserably. "That is, if Frank doesn't shoot me first."

"Nobody's shooting you," Rourke assured her.

"You can bet on that," Chet said.

Brenda smiled at them. "Thanks. She's my best friend."

Cappie hugged her. "Thanks anyway, for trying. I'll call you. See you, Kate!"

Kate waved as she picked up the ringing telephone. Her eyes were still on Rourke, who grinned at her.

"Come on, let's go," Cappie told the men.

"How's Kell?" Brenda asked, walking them out.

"He's going to make it. We won't know if he can walk for several days, though."

"If you have to go home, I'll visit him for you."

"I can't leave just yet," Cappie said. "Not until we find Frank."

Brenda stared at Bentley, who was all smiles. "Aren't you going back to your practice?"

"When we find Frank," he commented pleasantly.

"You're not part of this bodyguard unit," Chet reminded him.

"I am now," Bentley assured him. His eyes smoothed over Cappie. "I'm in it until the end."

Cappie hated the rush of pleasure that comment gave her. So she disguised it by hugging Brenda and promising to keep in touch.

CHAPTER NINE

BENTLEY WENT WITH them back to the hotel where Cappie was staying. He left them at the desk to get a room for himself. He managed one on the same floor, two doors down, and then went back to the other hotel where he'd been staying to pack his bags and check out.

"Great," Cappie muttered when they were back in her suite. "Now we're really going to be a parade."

"He likes you," Rourke pointed out. "And at this point, the more eyes, the better. He might see something we'd miss. After all, he knows what Frank looks like. We only have a mug shot. And you said it didn't really look much like him," he added, because he'd shown it to her earlier.

"All right," she sighed. She moved to the window and looked down at the busy street. "At least Kell's in good hands. I wouldn't want to walk in on Kilraven, even if he was in a good mood, with evil intent."

"There's an odd bird," Rourke commented. "We can't even find out which branch of the government he really works for, and we've tried. His brother works for the FBI, but Kilraven's true affiliations are less obvious."

She turned to him. "Is he CIA?"

"If he was, he wouldn't say so. And just for the record," he added with a grin, "no CIA office address is ever listed, in any city where we have offices. We don't even mention which cities those are."

"What a shadowy bunch you are," she commented.

He just grinned. "That's why we're so good at what we do."

"What we *do?*" she asked, hitting on the obvious assumption.

"I didn't say I was still with them," he pointed out.

"You didn't say you weren't, either," she replied.

He made a face at her.

"At least my job is up-front and everybody knows what it is," Chet said.

They both looked at him with wide eyes.

He glared at them. "I'm a bodyguard!"

"Well, so am I, right now," Rourke said. "But it's not what I do full-time." He gave the other man a narrow-eyed appraisal. "And it isn't what you do full-time, either."

Chet looked uncomfortable.

"What does he do full-time?" Cappie asked, curious.

"It involves long-range rifles and black ops."

"It does not," Chet muttered.

"It used to."

"Well, after I broke my leg, I was less enthusiastic about jumping out of Blackhawks," he muttered.

"You broke both legs, I heard."

Chet sighed. "And an arm. Breaks never heal properly, even with good medical care." He sighed again. "You try getting good medical care in..." He caught himself and closed his mouth.

"I wasn't going to say a word," Rourke told him.

"Well, don't. I'm out of cigarettes. I'm going down the street and see if I can find anybody in the mob to sell me a pack under the table, if the police aren't looking."

"Smoking's not illegal, is it?" Cappie asked.

"Any day now, it probably will be," Chet said despondently. "Can't spit without a federal permit these days," he said, and kept muttering all the way out the door.

"Quick, tell me," Cappie said to Rourke, "was he a sniper?"

"I've never been sure," he told her with a grin. "But he and Cash Grier are pretty chummy."

"Should that mean something?"

"Grier was a high-level government assassin in his younger days, but I didn't tell you that," he said firmly. "Some secrets have to be kept to save one's skin."

"Well!" she exclaimed. "I'd never have guessed."

"Neither would most other people. I'm going down the hall to loiter and see if I see anybody I recognize. Keep the door locked and don't answer it unless you recognize my voice, or Chet's. Got that?"

She nodded. "Thanks."

"When I do a job, I do a job," he told her. He closed the door behind him when he left.

SHE WAS JUMPY. With her protection, she shouldn't have been, but she kept remembering her last sight of Frank Bartlett, cursing her for all he was worth when the judge announced his sentence. He'd been yelling vengeance at the top of his lungs, and he'd almost managed to get away from the sheriff's deputy who had him in handcuffs. It had been a scary moment. Almost as scary as the memory of the night he'd beaten her.

She wrapped her arms around her rib cage and closed her eyes. She did hope they'd catch him before he got to her. Surely the job he'd done on Kell would guarantee him some quality prison time. But what if he got out again, after that? Would she have to live her entire life being afraid of Frank? After all, he could get out on good behavior, no matter how long his sentence was. Or he could hang a jury at his next trial. Or he could break out of prison. There were plenty of horrible possibilities, all of which would leave Cappie hiding behind locked doors as long as she lived. It wasn't a possibility she looked forward to.

The sudden knock on the door brought a cry of panic to her lips. She moved toward the door, but she didn't touch the knob. "Who…is it?" she called.

"Room service. We're checking to see if your veterinarian has been delivered yet."

She burst out laughing. She knew that curt voice, as well as she knew her own. "Bentley!" She moved closer to the door. "I don't recall ordering a veterinarian."

"Well, we're delivering one to you anyway, just in case you regret not ordering him later," he drawled.

She unlocked the door and gave him a droll look. "Nice tactics."

He shrugged. "I'm desperate. You wouldn't let me in if I just asked." He looked behind her and the smile faded. "Where are your bodyguards?"

"Chet went looking for cigarettes and Rourke is down the hall checking for intruders."

"And you're in here alone."

"Well, the door was locked until you asked to come in," she pointed out.

"Fair enough. Want to come downstairs and have coffee and pie with me? Then we can go to see Kell."

"I guess that would be okay. But I have to tell Rourke where I'm going…"

"He already knows," came an amused voice from the general direction of her purse.

"How did you get in here?" she asked, lifting the purse.

"I hid a microphone in there earlier, in case you escaped."

"I'm going downstairs to have coffee and pie, then Bentley and I are going to see Kell."

"Okay. I'll be around. Have fun. And don't hit him with the pie. You will be going to a hospital."

"On your way to a hospital is the best time to hit people with things," she retorted. "There are doctors there."

"Yes, I know," Bentley spoke into her purse. "I am one."

"You're a veterinarian," Rourke shot back.

"I can treat injuries if I want to."

"Try not to let her give you any."

"You stop that," Cappie told her purse. Nobody answered. "Hello?" she said, looking inside it.

"Don't do that in public, okay?" Bentley asked as they walked to the door. "There are probably psychiatrists around the hospital, too."

She rolled her eyes and went out into the hall just ahead of him.

THE HOSPITAL CAFETERIA was crowded. They found a table, but they had to share it with an elderly couple who'd come all the way from the Mexican border to visit their daughter, who'd just had a baby. They had photographs, and showed every single one to Bentley and Cappie, who made the correct responses between sips of coffee and bites of apple pie.

Finally the elderly couple finished their soft drinks and went off toward the elevator.

"Alone at last," Bentley teased.

"One more photograph would have done me in," she confessed. "I swear, if I ever have a grand-child…"

"…you'll have even more photos than they did, and show them to total strangers, too," he chuckled.

She shrugged and smiled. "Yes. I guess I would."

"Babies are nice. I used to think I'd like one or two, myself."

"You don't anymore?" she asked.

He moved his coffee mug around on the table. "I sort of gave up hope. Until you came along." He didn't look at her as he said it.

She felt her toes tingle. She hated the rush of pleasure she felt. "Really?"

He looked up. His pale blue eyes made sparks as they met hers. "Really."

She hesitated.

"I never should have believed a man I just met, who sat in my office and told lies about you with perfect innocence. But, then, I was afraid you were too good to be true."

"Nobody's perfect."

"I realize that. You don't have to be perfect. I just don't want to get in over my head and get kicked in the teeth again."

"I'm not that sort of person," she told him.

His eyes narrowed on her face. "He really hurt you, didn't he?"

"I thought I loved him," she said quietly. "He seemed to be kind and considerate…but the first date we had, he kicked my cat. I should have known then. Kind people aren't cruel to animals, ever. I found out later that he'd been abusive to at least two other women he dated, but they were too afraid of him to press charges." She smiled wanly. "Well, so was I. But Kell insisted. He said that Frank might end up killing someone if I didn't have him prosecuted. Then I'd have it on my conscience. I just didn't realize that it might be me that Frank killed." She put her face in her hands. "It won't ever end. Even if he goes back to trial, he could get off, or they could release him for good behavior, or he could break out…I'll never be free of him as long as I live."

"Don't talk like that," he said softly. "I won't let him hurt you."

She took her hands away. She looked older. "What if he hurt you? What if he killed you?

Anybody around me will be a target. I almost put Brenda in danger without even realizing it."

"I'm not afraid of the little weasel," he told her. "And you're not going to be afraid of him, either. That's how he controls women. With fear. Don't give him a foothold in your mind."

She bit her lip. "I'm just scared, Bentley."

"Yes, but you did the right thing. And you'll do it again, anytime you have to. You aren't the type of person who runs from trouble, any more than I am."

"You think so?"

"I know so."

She searched his eyes. "I was scared to death of you, at first. Then I was in a wreck and you drove me home." She smiled. "You aren't as horrible as you seem."

"Thanks. I think." He smiled back.

"Okay. I'll stick it out. If Frank escapes another jail sentence, maybe I can get Rourke to hide him in a jungle overseas, so deep that he'd never find his way out."

"Ahem," her purse replied, "I do not kidnap American citizens and carry them out of the country for nefarious purposes. Not even for pretty women."

"Spoilsport," she told him.

"However, I know people who would," he added, with a smile in his voice.

"Good man," Bentley said.

"Why don't you marry him?" Rourke asked. "At least he'd make sure you were never in harm's way."

"If you'll give me your boss's telephone number," Bentley told the purse, "I'll call him and give you a glowing recommendation."

"What a pal!"

"I always…"

Bentley stopped talking because three people were standing at their table with open mouths, watching him speak into Cappie's purse. He cleared his throat. "There, the radio's turned off now," he said in a deep, deliberate tone. He handed her back the purse.

The three people looked sheepish, smiled and left the cafeteria in a bit of a rush.

Cappie burst out laughing. Bentley's cheeks were the color of bubble gum.

"Quick thinking, there, Dr. Rydel," Rourke called over the radio. "Want to come work for us?"

"Go away," Cappie told him. "I am not going to consider marrying anybody in your line of work."

"Spoilsport," Rourke said. "Shutting up now."

Cappie met Bentley's eyes, and they both laughed.

KELL WAS GROGGY and quiet. The pain must have been pretty bad, Cappie thought, once the anesthetic wore off. He was much less talkative than he'd been when he was just out of the recovery room. He was pale and he looked as if it was an effort to say anything at all. They only stayed a couple of minutes. Kell was asleep before they got out the door.

"Do you think it would be safe to step outside just for a minute and get a breath of air?" Cappie asked. "There are people everywhere."

"I don't know," Bentley said, his eyes roving.

"Rourke, what do you think?" she asked her purse.

But there was no reply. She looked around. She didn't see Rourke or Chet. That was odd. They'd been visible every minute since she came to San Antonio.

"Maybe it would be all right," she said. "I just want to stretch my legs for a minute."

"All right," Bentley said. "But you stay close to me." He slid his big hand into her small one and closed it warmly. "I'll take care of you."

She smiled wearily and laid her head against his shoulder for a minute. "Okay."

They walked out into the cold night air. The sidewalk was crowded. Traffic passed by. There was a policeman on the corner, leaning back against a storefront, talking into a cell phone. Nearby, two men in suits were talking, oblivious to passersby.

All around them, neon signs and holiday lights brightened the darkness. "It's almost Christmas," she exclaimed. "With all that's happened, I forgot." She grimaced. "We won't get to open presents under the tree this year. Kell will never be able to go home by Christmas Eve."

"Then we'll put up a small tree in his room and transfer the presents up here from Jacobsville," he promised her. "We'll have Christmas here."

She looked up at him with soft, quiet eyes. "We?"

His jaw tautened. "I'm not leaving you again. Not even for a day," he said huskily.

The words made tears brim in her eyes. The way he said it was so poignant, so passionate. He didn't even need to say what he was feeling. She read it in his face.

He pulled her into his arms and held her close, hugged her tight, buried his face in her long, soft hair. "Marry me."

She closed her eyes. "Yes. Yes!" she whispered.

His chest rose and fell heavily. "Of all the places

to get engaged," he groaned. "With a thousand eyes watching."

"It doesn't matter," she whispered.

No, he thought. It didn't.

"Hold him! I'll get her!"

The voices came suddenly into what was the sweetest dream of Cappie's life. She was so relaxed, so happy, that it took precious seconds for her to realize what was about to happen. She felt Bentley torn from her arms. Two men were pulling his arms behind him. A violent jerk brought her around as two bruising hands caught her shoulders and twisted them. Above her, Frank Bartlett's angry, contorted features came into view, his narrow dark eyes promising retribution.

"Got you at last, didn't I?" he growled. "Now, you're going to pay for what you did to me!"

She cried out and tried to pull away from him, but his hands were too strong. He drew one back and slapped her as hard as he could, so hard that she staggered and would have fallen if he hadn't jerked her back up brutally with the other hand.

Her face stung like fire. There would be a bruise. But it only made her mad. She drew back her high-heeled foot and kicked him in the calf muscle as hard as she could. He yelled in pain and slapped her again. But before he could draw back another time, he suddenly went down under a vicious tackle.

"That's the way, brother!" came a cheering cry from the sidelines.

"Go get him!" came another hearty voice.

Bentley was knocking the stuffing out of Frank Bartlett, his big fists making the other man, a match for him pound for pound, cry out in pain.

"Now isn't he talented?" Rourke murmured as he drew a shaky Cappie back from the crowd. He looked at her bruised face and winced. "Sorry we didn't rush right in, but we wanted to make sure we had plenty of witnesses and an excellent case for the prosecution." He jerked his head toward Chet and the two men in suits. They had the two men with Frank subdued and handcuffed. The uniformed officer who'd been on the corner was standing with them.

"We had you staked out," Rourke told her. "I wouldn't have done it this way, if there had been any other choice."

She reached up and patted his cheek. "You did good, Dead-Eye," she said with a smile, and winced when it hurt. "I'm going to look like an accident victim for a few days, I'm afraid."

"No doubt about that. Your poor face!"

She glanced back toward Frank. Bentley was still pounding him. "Shouldn't you save Bentley?"

"Bentley?" he exclaimed.

"From a homicide charge, I mean," she clarified.

"Oh. Right. Probably should."

He moved forward and pulled Bentley off the other man. It took some doing. The veterinarian was obviously reluctant to give up his pastime.

"Now, now," Rourke calmed him, "we have to have enough left to prosecute. Besides, Cappie needs some TLC. She's pretty bruised."

Bentley was catching his breath as he walked quickly back to Cappie. He winced at the sight of her face. "My poor baby," he exclaimed, bending to kiss her bruised cheek with exquisite tenderness. "Let me just go back over there and hit him one more time…!"

"No," she protested, grabbing his suit coat. "Rourke's right, we have to have enough of him left to prosecute. Bentley, you were magnificent!"

"So were you, kicking him in the leg," he chuckled.

"I guess we make a pretty good team," she mused.

"You can say that again."

She put a hand to her cheek. "Boy, that stings."

"It looks like hell. You'll have to see a doctor."

"Fortunately there are plenty of those right inside," Rourke came back in time to reply. "See the letters? They spell out *hospital*."

She drew back a fist.

Rourke held up both hands. "Now, now, I'm on your side." He nodded toward one of the men in suits who had a long black ponytail. "Recognize him?"

She frowned. "No…"

"That's Detective Sergeant Rick Marquez," he told her. "He was just on his way to the opera when we phoned and said an assault with intent was going down in front of the hospital. He broke speed records getting here."

"How kind of him," Cappie said.

"Not really. He always goes to the opera alone. He can't get women."

"But, why not?" she wondered. "He's a dish."

"He carries a gun," Rourke pointed out.

"You carry a gun."

"I can't get women, either."

"What a shame."

He moved closer. "I'm available."

She laughed as Bentley stepped in front of her, glowering.

"Wait, scratch that, I just remembered, I'm not available," Rourke said quickly.

"Even if you were, she's not," Bentley said.

"There you are, again, starting trouble," Rick Marquez chuckled, joining them. He looked at Cappie's face and grimaced. "Damn, I'm sorry we didn't get here sooner," he apologized. "I couldn't get a cab and I had to run all the way."

"Fortunately you're in great shape," Rourke said.

"Fortunately I am," Marquez agreed. "What are you and Billings doing here?"

"Trading favors with Eb Scott." Rourke grinned. "We're bodyguards. Well, not anymore. Not now that you have those three jackals in custody."

Marquez moved a step closer to him. "How about telling Chet that he's not allowed to smoke here?"

"Why don't you tell him?" Rourke asked, surprised.

"Too many windows overlook my apartment," came the amused reply. "He might not be able to resist the temptation to get even."

"Good point. I'll just pass that along. About the smoking!" Rourke added quickly. "Anyway, he wouldn't shoot you. He's not sanctioned."

"Yet," Marquez enunciated.

Rourke shrugged, grinned and went to find his partner.

"They really were great," Cappie told the detective. "I've never felt safer. Well, until tonight."

"We let you walk into the trap," Marquez replied quietly. "It was the only way we could guarantee a case against Bartlett that he couldn't escape. His sort doesn't give up."

"Yes, but he could get out again…"

"He won't," Marquez said curtly. "I promise you that. See that guy I was standing with? He's the assistant D.A. who put Frank away in the first place."

"I thought he looked familiar," Cappie returned.

"He cursed a blue streak because the judge gave him such an easy sentence. He's been working behind the scenes to get depositions in case Frank slipped." He grinned. "And did Frank ever slip! In front of all these witnesses, too." He indicated the uniformed officer, and two others who'd joined him, who were questioning bystanders. "Frank is going back in jail for a long time."

"What about his friends?" Cappie asked.

"I know what they helped him do to your brother. We couldn't have proved it, before, but I'm betting one of them will be happy to turn state's evidence in return for a reduced sentence."

"Meanwhile," Bentley said, sliding an affectionate arm around Cappie, "we're going to have a nice Christmas celebration with Kell in the hospital and then plan a wedding."

"A wedding?" Marquez sighed. "I used to think I'd find a nice woman someday who liked cops and opera, who'd love to marry me. But, I'm really happy to be single. I mean, I have all sorts of free time, and I get to watch whatever television programs I like, and TV dinners are just wonderful. In fact, I think I might like to do commercials for them." He smiled.

"They have psychiatrists in there, don't they?" Bentley asked, nodding toward the hospital.

Marquez glared at him. "I'm happy, I said! I love living alone! I never want my private life messed up by some sweet, loving woman who can cook!"

"Anybody got a straitjacket?" Bentley asked.

Marquez threw up his hands and walked away.

Cappie felt her face begin to throb. Tears stung her eyes. "Could we go back inside and find the emergency room, you think?" she asked Bentley.

"Right this minute," he said with obvious concern.

Marquez followed them inside. "I've got my digital camera with me," he said, suddenly all business. "We want to get photos, to make sure a jury sees what Frank did to you."

"Be my guest," Cappie replied. "But then I want aspirin and an ice pack!"

"You can come down to my office in the morning to give me a statement. For now, we'll get the photos and have a doctor look at your face. After that, you can even have a beer if you like, and I'll buy," Marquez promised.

She made a face. "Sorry, but I'd rather have the ice pack."

Bentley's arm contracted. "Then we have to find some way to keep Kell from seeing your poor face, until he's through the worst of his own ordeal."

"Yes, we do," she said. "That isn't going to be easy."

Marquez, seeing the bruising increase by the second, had to agree. And she didn't know yet how it was going to look a day later. But he did.

THEY DID TAKE X-rays of Cappie's face. Marquez got his photos and left. The doctor treating her came back into the cubicle where she and Bentley were waiting in the busy emergency room.

"There are two small broken bones," he said. "I want you to take these X-rays to your primary physician and let him refer you to a good plastic surgeon. Meanwhile, I'm going to write you something for pain. Keep ice on the swelling. Nothing is going to disguise the bruises, I'm afraid." He glanced curiously at Bentley.

"I didn't do it," Bentley said easily. "The man who did was taken away in a squad car, with his accomplices, and he's going to be prosecuted to the full extent of the law. Those X-rays we asked for a copy of are going to help put him away."

The young resident nodded somberly. "I see far too many injuries like this. A boyfriend?" he queried.

"No," Cappie said heavily. "An ex-boyfriend who spent six months in jail for breaking my arm," she added. "He got out and came looking for me. This time, I hope he'll stay as a guest of the state for much longer."

"I'll be happy to testify," the resident said. He pulled a card out of his wallet and handed it to her. "That happens too often, you know, a brutal man seeking revenge. We had a young woman killed a few weeks ago for the same thing."

Cappie felt sick to her stomach.

Bentley put his arm around her. "Nobody's killing you," he said.

She leaned her head against him. "Thanks."

They took the extra X-ray in its envelope, paid the bill and left the emergency room, hand-in-hand.

"Do you want to go and see Kell tonight?" Bentley asked.

She shook her head, wincing, because it hurt. "I'm too sick. I just want to lie down." She looked up. "Will you go with me to Marquez's office in the morning?"

"You'd better believe I will."

"Thanks."

His arm contracted around her. "Not necessary. Let's get you back to your room. It's been a long day."

"Tell me about it," she mused. At least, she thought, her ordeal was over for the moment. Tomorrow she could worry about the details, including telling poor Kell what had happened.

CHAPTER TEN

CAPPIE GROANED AT her own reflection in the hotel mirror when she climbed out of bed the next morning. One whole side of her face was a brilliant purple, and swollen to boot.

"You okay in there?"

She smiled. Bentley had insisted on sleeping on the sofa in the suite, just in case. Rourke and Chet were already up and packing their things for the trip back to Jacobsville. Cappie and Bentley were staying for another day or two, while she gave statements to the police and looked after Kell.

"I think so," she said. "I just can't bear to look at myself."

"I'll bet Chet knows exactly how that feels!" Rourke called from the doorway of the room he and Chet had shared.

"Will you shut up?" Chet muttered.

"Now, that's a good example of how much work your diplomatic skills need," Rourke admonished.

"I'm through trying to be diplomatic," Chet said curtly. "I'm going back to the company and let them send me off on lone assignments, all by myself. Anywhere I don't have to try to be nice to people!"

"Yes, and you can take those smokes with you," Rourke added. "Having to share a room with you is punishment enough for any lawbreaker! Man, you reek!"

"Cigarette smoke is beneficial," Chet told him.

"It is not!"

"If your quarry smokes, you can smell him from five hundred meters," Chet returned, and he actually smiled.

Rourke's jaw dropped. He'd never seen the other man smile.

Chet gave him a haughty, arrogant stare, picked up his bag and walked out. "Hope things go well for you, Miss Drake," he said as she came out of her room wrapped in a thick robe. He winced. "It will look much better in a week or so," he assured her.

She tried to smile, but it hurt too much. "Thanks for helping keep me alive, Chet."

"My pleasure. See you back at Scott's place, Rourke."

"You wait for me—I'm not paying cab fare back to Jacobsville all alone," Rourke said. He picked up his own bag, shook hands with Bentley and bent to kiss Cappie's undamaged cheek. "If he ever walks out on you, just get word to me, and I'll bring him back to you in a net," he said in a stage whisper.

"Thanks, Rourke. But I don't think that will ever happen."

Bentley smiled. "I can guarantee it won't."

"Cheers, then. See you."

They waved the two men off. Bentley studied her poor, damaged face warily. "I wish there had been some way to prevent that."

"Me, too. But it's insurance. Let's get breakfast. Then we can go down to Detective Marquez's office and start giving statements. Later," she added reluctantly, "we can go see Kell and try not to upset him too much when we tell him what happened."

"Suits me."

DETECTIVE MARQUEZ HAD a small office in a big department. It was noisy and people seemed to come and go constantly. The phones rang off the hook.

"This looks like those crime shows on television," Cappie remarked.

Marquez chuckled. "It's much worse. You can't get five minutes' peace to type up a report." He got up to retrieve the report he'd typed at the computer as he questioned her. He took it out of the printer tray and handed it to her. "Check over that, if you will, and see if I've got it right." He pulled out another one. "This one's for you, Dr. Rydel." He handed the vet another sheet of paper.

They went over their statements, made a couple of corrections. Marquez inserted the corrections and printed the statements out again. They signed them.

"I'll bet Frank's foaming at the mouth," Cappie mused.

"He really is, but this time he's not going to fool any jury into thinking he's the injured party," Marquez assured her.

"I'll bet that judge is feeling bad about now," Bentley muttered.

"The judge did feel bad," Marquez agreed. "So did the district attorney, especially after Frank and his cohorts beat up your brother. The whole justice system here in San Antonio went into overdrive to catch the perp."

"Really?" Cappie asked, surprised.

"Really. The assistant district attorney who prosecuted your case was in the vanguard."

"Somebody needs to take him out for a big steak dinner," Cappie commented.

"I'm taking him out for one, at my mother's café in Jacobsville," he chuckled. "Of course, he's eligible and so is my mother."

"I see wheels turning in your head," Cappie said.

He grinned. "Always," Marquez said easily. "He and I have worked several cases together. I like him."

"Me, too," Cappie said. She hesitated. "Frank won't get out until the trial, will he?"

Marquez shook his head. "The assistant D.A. is having the bond set in the six-figure range. I don't think Frank knows a bail bondsman who'll take a chance on him for that amount of money."

"Let's hope not," Bentley said.

Marquez gave him a keen glance. "He'll probably stay in jail voluntarily, to keep from having you come at him again. That was some tackle."

Bentley shrugged. "I used to play football in college."

"I played soccer. Don't get to do much tackling, but I can knock a ball half a block with my head."

"Is that why it looks that way?" a familiar voice drawled from the cubicle doorway.

"Kilraven," Marquez grumbled, "will you stop stalking me?"

"I'm not stalking you," the tall man said easily. "I'm just waiting for you to answer my ten phone calls, six voice mails and twenty e-mails." He glowered at the younger man.

Marquez held up his hands. "Okay. Just let me finish up with Miss Drake and Dr. Rydel and I'll be right with you. Honest."

"No hurry," Kilraven said, smiling. "I'll be standing right out here, intimidating lawbreakers."

"Thanks for looking out for Kell," Cappie told him.

"What are friends for?" he asked.

"How would you know, Kilraven, you don't have any friends," a passing detective drawled.

"I have lots of friends!"

"Oh, yeah? Name one."

"Marquez!"

"He's your friend?" the detective asked Marquez, sticking his head into the cubicle.

"He is not," Marquez said without looking up as he glanced over the statements one last time.

"I am so," Kilraven said in a surly tone.

Marquez gave him a speaking glance.

Kilraven moved back out of the cubicle, muttering to himself in some foreign language.

"I know what that means in Arabic," Marquez called after him. "Your brother speaks Farsi fluently and he taught me what those words mean!"

A rolling barrage in yet another language came lilting into the cubicle.

"What's that?" Marquez asked.

Kilraven poked his head in and grinned, "Lakota. And Jon can't teach you that—he doesn't speak it. Ha!"

He left.

Marquez grimaced.

"He's really very nice," Cappie said.

Marquez leaned toward her. "He is, but I'm not saying it out loud." His expression became somber. "I'm working on a cold case with him and another detective," he said quietly. "It involves him. He's impatient, because we got a new lead."

Bentley nodded quietly. "I know about that one. One of my vet techs is married to the best friend of our local sheriff. I hear most of what's going on."

"Tragic case," Marquez agreed. "But hopefully we're going to crack it."

Bentley got to his feet, tugging Cappie up with him. He winced as she turned toward him.

"I appreciate the copies of those X-rays," Marquez added, walking out with them. "Everything we can throw against Bartlett will help put him away."

"He'd better hope he never gets out," Cappie said. "My brother will be waiting for him if he does."

Marquez chuckled. "If it hadn't been three to one against, and your brother hadn't been in a wheelchair, I'd probably be helping defend him on homicide charges."

"No doubt," Bentley replied somberly.

Cappie frowned. "Is there a conversation going on that I don't know anything about?" she asked.

Bentley and Marquez exchanged covert glances. "Just commenting on your brother's justifiable anger," Bentley told her easily. He caught her fingers in his. "Let's go see your brother and tell him he's about to have a new brother-in-law."

KELL WAS A little better, until he saw Cappie's face. He swore brilliantly.

"I know how you feel," Bentley said. "But for what it's worth, Bartlett probably looks much worse. It took two detectives to pull me off him."

Kell brightened. "Good man." He winced at his sister's face, though. "I'm so sorry."

"I'll heal." She didn't mention the potential surgery she might have to undergo. There was no need to worry him even more. "Detective Marquez said that Frank won't get out for a long time. He expects one of Frank's accomplices to turn state's evidence. If they charge him with battery on both of us, he'll do some serious time."

"I expected Hayes Carson to show up here and ask me for a statement for what Frank did to me in Comanche Wells," he murmured.

"I imagine he's giving you time to get over the surgery," Cappie said.

"Probably so."

"Have you spoken to the surgeon yet?" Cappie asked.

He smiled. "Yes. He's optimistic, especially since I have feeling in my legs now."

"At least something good may come out of all this misery," she said gently.

Kell was looking at Bentley. "Just before we came up here to the hospital, she said she didn't want to live in a town that also contained you. You told me part of the story, but not any more than you had to. She was going to explain, then they knocked me out with a shot. Care to comment?"

"I made a stupid decision," Bentley said with a sigh. "I expect to be apologizing for it for the rest of my life. But she's going to marry me anyway."

He gave her a tender smile, which she returned. "I can eat crow at every meal, for however long it takes."

"I stopped being mad at you while you were beating the stuffing out of Frank Bartlett," she pointed out.

He glanced at his bruised, swollen knuckles. "I'll have permanent mementoes of the occasion, I expect."

"You're getting married?" Kell asked.

"Yes," Cappie said. She touched her face gingerly. "Not until the swelling goes down, though."

"And not until I'm able to walk down the aisle and give you away," Kell interjected.

Bentley pursed his lips. "I could get Chet and Rourke to carry you down the aisle to give her away," he offered.

"The last wedding Chet went to, he spent the night in jail for inciting a riot," Kell pointed out.

Cappie frowned. "Exactly how well do you know Chet and Rourke?" she asked pointedly.

He groaned. "Oh. The pain. I need to rest. I really can't talk anymore right now."

Cappie's eyes narrowed on the drip catheter. "Doesn't that thing automatically inject painkiller into the drip while you're post-surgical?" she asked.

Kell kept his eyes closed. "I don't know. I feel terrible. You have to leave now." He opened one eye. "You can come back later, when I'll be much better as long as you don't ask potentially embarrassing questions. If you do, I may have a relapse."

"All right," Cappie sighed.

He brightened. "Be good and I'll tell you how to get past the Hunters in ODST."

"Cash told you?" she asked.

He chuckled and winced, because moving hurt. "Not without a bribe."

"What sort of bribe?"

"Remember that old Bette Davis movie, where she murders her lover and then has to blackmail the man's widow over a letter that could convict her?" he asked.

"Yes. It's called *The Letter*…it's one of my favorite…" She stopped. "You didn't!"

"Hey, it's not as if you watch it that much," Kell protested.

"Kell!"

"Do you want to get past the Hunters, or don't you?" he asked.

She sighed. "I guess I can always find another copy of it somewhere."

"That's a nice sister," Kell said.

"If I buy you another one," Bentley interrupted,

"will you tell *me* how to get past the Hunters?" he asked her.

They all laughed.

TWO WEEKS LATER, Kell was walking down the hall, wobbling a little, in his pajamas and robe while Cappie held him up. The swelling in her cheek had gone down, but it still had a yellowish tinge to it. Kell was much better. He was learning how to walk all over again, courtesy of the rehab department in the Jacobsville hospital.

"This is slow," he muttered.

"It is not," Bentley retorted, and the sound of gunfire came from the television in the living room. "Ha! That's one Hunter down!"

"Rub it in," she called. "It wasn't even your favorite movie you had to sacrifice to learn how to do that!"

"I bought you a new one. It's in the DVD player," he called back.

"Fat lot of good it's doing me, since that game console hasn't been off for five minutes all day," she muttered.

"Stop picking on my future brother-in-law," Kell chided. "It isn't every man who can make tortillas from scratch."

"He only did it to butter you up," she told him.

"It worked. When's the wedding, again?"

"Three weeks from now. Micah Steele says you'll be able to manage the church aisle with just a cane by then. And we can hope there won't be a large animal emergency anywhere in the county during the ceremony!" she raised her voice.

"I'm borrowing a vet from San Antonio to cover the practice for me until we're back from our honeymoon in Cancún," he said. They'd picked the exotic spot because it had been the dream of Cappie's life to see Chichen Itza, the Mayan ruin.

"I hope the vet knows he's covering for you," she said.

He chuckled. "He does."

"The guest list just keeps growing," Cappie sighed. "I've already sent out fifty invitations."

"Did you put Marquez and the assistant D.A. on the list?"

"Yes," she said. "And Rourke and Chet, too."

Kell groaned.

"Chet won't start any riots. I'll have a talk with him," she promised. "They took good care of me in San Antonio," she added.

"Yes, but I was the one who took down Frank," Bentley called. "Can you believe that little weasel tried to sue me for assault?" he added huffily.

"He didn't get as far as first base," Kell assured

him. "Blake Kemp had a long talk with his attorney."

"Why would our D.A. be talking to a defense attorney in San Antonio?" Cappie wanted to know.

"Because the defense attorney wasn't aware of the familial connections of the defendant's assailant," Bentley murmured. "Ha! There went another Hunter!" he exclaimed.

Cappie blinked. "Familial connections…?"

Kell leaned down to her ear. "Don't ask. The upshot is that the lawsuit is going nowhere. Fast."

Cappie was still staring at Bentley. "What familial connections?" she persisted.

"The governor is my first cousin. Ha! Another one!"

"Our governor?" she exclaimed.

"We only have one. This game is great!"

Cappie sighed. She looked up at her handsome big brother. "The game is not going with us on our honeymoon," she said firmly.

Bentley gave her a roguish glance. "Not even if I tell you how to get past the Hunters?"

"Well, in that case, maybe I could reconsider," she chuckled.

KELL DID MAKE it down the aisle with a cane. The little country church in Comanche Wells was filled to capacity. Only people they knew got an invitation, but there was still standing room only. A good many of the guests were in uniform, either military or law enforcement, on one side of the church, while a number of Eb Scott's guys were seated across the aisle from them. Covert glares were exchanged. Down the center aisle marched Cappie in her lovely white gown with what seemed acres of lace and a pretty fingertip veil. She was carrying a bouquet of yellow roses and wearing a smile that went from ear to ear.

She held on to Kell's arm tightly, so proud of his progress that she beamed with happiness. He was already talking about a new job working for Eb Scott at his anti-terrorism school. She was really curious about how well her brother seemed to know any number of Eb's employees, but she hadn't made any comments. She was still indebted to Eb for lending her Chet and Rourke, who were seated together in the front of the church. Around them were her former and present coworkers, including Keely and Boone Sinclair. Boone's sister, Winnie, was being watched with real intensity by Kilraven, dressed in an expensive suit in the row behind her.

She and Kell stopped at the altar, where he gave her hand to Bentley. He was beaming, too, so handsome that Cappie just sighed, looking up at him with gray eyes that adored him.

The wedding service was brief, but poignant. Bentley lifted the veil and bent to kiss her with such tenderness that she had to fight tears.

Then he led her down the aisle to the back of the church. The people who hadn't been able to squeeze into the church were waiting outside with what seemed like buckets of rice and confetti. They were totally drenched in both as they ran to the white limousine that was to take them to the town civic center, for the reception.

THEY FED EACH other cake, posed for wedding pictures and generally had a wonderful time. There was a live band and they danced together to a slow, romantic tune, which lasted for all of two minutes before Cash Grier, with his beautiful wife, Tippy, signaled to the band leader.

There were grins, a fanfare and then a furious and delicious rendition of the classic tune "Brazil." But Cash didn't start dancing, as everyone expected him to. He glanced toward Bentley with a chuckle and a flourish.

Bentley gave Cappie a wicked look. "Shall we?"

"But, Bentley, you can't dance...can you?" she exclaimed.

"I couldn't," he confessed, taking her onto the dance floor. "But Cash gave me lessons. Okay. One, two...three!"

He twirled her around in the most professional sort of way, in a mixture of samba, cha-cha and mambo that she followed with consummate ease while people on the sidelines began to clap.

"You're terrific!" Cappie panted.

"So are you, gorgeous," he chuckled. "Are we good, or what?"

About a day and a half later, they repeated the same exact dialog to each other, but for a totally different reason.

Lying exhausted and bathed in sweat in a huge double bed in a beachfront hotel in Cancún, they could barely move.

"And I thought you danced well!" she laughed. "You're just amazing!"

"Why, thank you," he drawled, grinning. "May I return the compliment?"

"Yes, well, I think I'm a quick study," she sighed.

"Not so nervous anymore, I notice," he murmured.

She laughed. She was almost a basket case of nerves when they checked into the hotel that afternoon. She loved Bentley, but she had no real idea of what it was going to be like when they were alone together. But he was understanding, patient and gentle as he cradled her in his arms in a big easy chair and fed her shrimp from a big platter of seafood that room service had brought up. Of course, he'd also fed her champagne in increasing amounts, until she was so relaxed that nothing he suggested seemed to disturb her.

Slow, tender kisses grew slower and more insistent. He coaxed her out of her clothing with such ease that she barely noticed until she felt the cool air on her skin. Even then, the way he was touching her was so electrifying that her only conscious thought was to see how much closer to him she could get. There was one little flash of pain, easily forgotten as he kissed her with delicate sensuality and lifted her back into the fiery hunger the hesitation had briefly interrupted. Her mind had gone into eclipse while her body demanded and pleaded for an end to the tension which he built in her so effortlessly. Finally, finally, she fell over the edge of it into a blazing heat of fulfillment that exceeded her wildest expectations.

"And I used to think you were reserved!" she laughed.

"Only when I'm wearing a white lab coat," he

murmured drowsily. He opened his eyes, rolled over and studied her pretty pink nudity with lazy appreciation. "Would you like me to get up and put on a lab coat, and be reserved?"

"I would not," she retorted, pulling him back down. She kissed him intensely. "I'd like you to be unreserved all over again, starting right now."

He slid over her, his hair-roughened chest grazing the hard tips of her pretty breasts. "I can't think of anything I'd enjoy more, Mrs. Rydel."

She would have answered him back, but she was much too involved for speech.

THEY WANDERED THROUGH the ruins at Chichen Itza hand in hand, fascinated as they strolled around the wide plain that contained the pyramidal Castillo and the other buildings that made up the Mayan complex.

"It must have looked much different when it was occupied, all those hundreds of years ago," Cappie mused, her eyes everywhere.

"There were probably even more people," he chuckled, glancing at the crowds of tourists that abounded, even this time of year. He handed her his huge water bottle and waited for her to take a sip before he followed suit. The bus trip here was hours long, and it would be after dark before they got back to their hotel. It was something they'd both wanted to see.

"It's a lot different, being here, than seeing it on television," she remarked.

"Most things are," he replied. "Until they can discover a way to let you touch and smell distant ruins, it won't be as much fun to watch it on a small screen."

She stopped and looked up at him with her heart in her gray eyes. "I never thought being married would be so much fun."

He hugged her close. "And we're only at the beginning of our marriage," he agreed, his blue eyes soft as they scanned her face. "I hope we have a hundred years ahead of us."

"Me, too." She pressed into his arms and closed her eyes. "Me, too, Bentley."

SHE WENT BACK to work for him in the practice. She'd argued that if Keely, who was happily married and well-off, could keep working, she could, too. He hadn't protested too much. It delighted him to be able to see her all day long.

"Don't you want a cat?" Keely coaxed the week after they came back from their honeymoon. "I've got six little white kittens that Grace Grier asked me to find homes for, and I've only placed four of them."

Cappie laughed. "I'd love one."

"Me, too," Bentley agreed, poking his head around the corner. "Did Cy Parks call back about that new bull of his that got cut on the barbed wire?"

"He did. He said if you'd drop by on your way home, he and Lisa would feed you both," Keely chuckled. "They're having homemade chili and corn bread."

"My favorite," Bentley said.

"Mine, too," Cappie replied almost at the same time as Bentley.

"He said you could bring Kell along," the other girl added.

"Kell's gone off somewhere with Rourke and Chet," Cappie sighed. "No telling where. They vanish for days at a time, and nobody knows where. He's my own brother. You'd think he could trust me."

"And me," Bentley added.

"I'm sure he has his reasons," Cappie said. "Whatever they are."

"It's bound to be something covert and dangerous and exciting," Keely said out loud.

"More than likely, they're helping Detective

Marquez stake out a nightclub or something," Bentley chuckled. "He did mention that he needed a couple of willing volunteers for a special project he and that assistant district attorney are working on."

"We owe that district attorney," Cappie agreed. "He talked Frank's accomplices into testifying against him for reduced sentences. He says Frank won't get out until his hair turns gray. Made my day," she added.

"Mine, too," Bentley assured her. "Okay, people, back to work."

"Yes, sir, Dr. Rydel, sir," Cappie said, saluting him.

He made a face at her. Then he grinned.

She grinned back, turning back to her coworker behind the counter. "Who's next, Keely?"

"Mrs. Anderson and her Chihuahua. Got the chart right here."

Cappie took it from her and went out into the waiting room, which was full. Her eyes were bright with happiness as she exchanged a glance with her handsome husband, just before he went into the back to examine a surgical patient. She felt as if she could walk on air.

"Okay, Mrs. Anderson," she told an elderly little woman with a smile. "If you'll bring Tweedle on back, we'll get Dr. Rydel to take a look at his bruised paw."

"He's a very nice doctor," the little woman told Cappie. "You're a lucky young woman!"

"Yes, you are!" Bentley called from the back. "Not every woman gets a husband who's as accomplished and modest as I am! You should be proud of yourself!"

"I am, dear, and how do you like your potatoes…burned or charbroiled?"

There was a pause. "Not every husband gets a wife as accomplished and modest as you are, dear!" he called back.

She chuckled. "Now that will get you a nice scalloped potato dish and a beautifully cooked pot roast!"

An amused Mrs. Anderson wiggled her eyebrows at Cappie as she followed her to a treatment room. Cappie just grinned.

* * * * *

*Read on for a glimpse of INVINCIBLE,
the latest from Diana Palmer,
in stores and online August 2014
wherever Harlequin books are sold!*

CHAPTER ONE

IT WAS A rainy Friday morning. Carlie Blair, who was running late for her job as Jacobsville, Texas, police chief Cash Grier's secretary, only had time for a piece of toast and a sip of coffee before she rushed out the door to persuade her ten-year-old red pickup truck to start. It had gone on grinding seemingly forever before, finally, the engine fired up. Her father the mechanic—and Methodist minister—was out of town on business for the day. So there was nobody to help her get it running. Luck was with her. It did, at last, start.

She envied her friend Michelle Godfrey, whose guardian and his sister had given her a Jaguar for Christmas. Michelle was away at college now, and she and Carlie still spoke on the phone, but they no longer shared rides to town, and gas, on a daily basis. The old clunker ate gas like candy and Carlie's salary only stretched so far.

She wished she had more than two pairs of jeans, six T-shirts, a coat and one good pair of shoes. It must be nice, she thought, not to have to count pennies. But her father was always optimistic about their status. *God loved the poor, because they gave away so much,* he was fond of saying. He was probably right. But her rain-wet jeans were uncomfortable, and she'd stepped in a mud puddle with her only pair of good shoes while she was knocking corrosion off the battery terminals with the hammer she kept under the front seat for that purpose. All this in January weather, which was wet and cold and miserable, even in south Texas.

Consequently, when she parked her car in the small lot next to the chief's office, she looked like a bedraggled rat. Her dark, short, wavy hair was curling like crazy, as it always did in a rainstorm. Her coat was soaked. Her green eyes, full of silent resignation, didn't smile as she opened the office door.

Her worst nightmare was standing just inside. Carson glared at her. He was so much taller that she had to look up at him. There was a lot to look at, although she tried not to show her interest. He was all muscle, but it wasn't overly obvious. He had a rodeo rider's physique, lean and powerful. Like her, he wore jeans, but his were obviously designer ones, like those hand-tooled leather boots on his big feet and the elaborately scrolled leather holster in which he kept his .45 automatic. He was wearing a jacket that partially concealed the gun, but he was intimidating enough without it.

He was Lakota Sioux. He had jet-black hair that fell to his waist in back, although he wore it in a ponytail usually. He had large black eyes that seemed to see everything with one sweep. He had high cheekbones and a light olive complexion. There were faint scars on the knuckles of his big hands. She noticed because he was holding a file in one of them. Her file. The chief's file that had been lying on her desk, waiting to be put in the computer. It referenced an attack on her father a few weeks earlier that had resulted in her being stabbed.

Involuntarily, her hand went to the scar that ran from her shoulder down to the beginning of her small breast. She flushed when she saw where he was looking.

"Those are confidential files," she said shortly.

He looked around. "There was nobody here to tell me that," he said, his deep voice clear as a bell in the silent room.

She flushed at the implied criticism. "Damned truck wouldn't start and I got soaked trying to get it going," she muttered. She slid her weather-beaten old purse under her desk, ran a hand through her wet hair, took off her ratty coat and hung it up before she sat down at her desk. "Did you need something?" she asked with crushing politeness. She even managed a smile. Sort of.

"I need to see the chief," he replied.

She frowned. "There's this thing called a door. He's got one," she said patiently. "You knock on it, and he comes out."

He gave her a look that could have stopped traffic. "There's somebody in there with him," he said with equal patience. "I didn't want to interrupt."

"I see." She moved things around on her desk, muttering to herself.

"Bad sign."

She looked up. "Huh?"

"Talking to yourself."

She glared at him. It had been a tough morning altogether and he wasn't helping. "Don't listen, if it bothers you."

He gave her a long look and laughed hollowly. "Listen, kid, nothing about you bothers me. Or ever will."

There was the sound of chairs scraping wood, as if the men in Cash's office had stood up. She figured it was safe to interrupt him. Well, safer than listening to Mr. Original American here run her down.

She pushed the intercom button. "You have a visitor, sir," she announced.

There was a murmur. "Who is it?"

She looked at Carson. "The gentlemen who starts fires with hand grenades," she said sweetly.

Carson stared at her with icy black eyes.

Cash's door opened, and there was Carlie's father, a man in a very expensive suit and Cash.

That explained why her father had left home so early. He was out of town, as he'd said he would be; out of Comanche Wells, where they lived, anyway. Not that Jacobsville was more than a five-minute drive from there.

"Carson," Cash said, nodding. "I think you know Reverend Blair and my brother Garon?"

"Yes." Carson shook hands with them.

Carlie was doing mental shorthand. Garon Grier was an assistant senior agent in charge of the Jacobsville branch of the FBI. He'd moved to Jacobsville some time ago, but the FBI branch office hadn't been here quite as long. Garon had been with the bureau for a very long time. Carlie wondered what was going on that involved both the FBI and her father. But she knew that question would go unanswered. Her father was remarkably silent on issues that concerned law enforcement, although he knew quite a few people in that profession.

She recalled with a chill the telephone conversation she'd recently had with someone who'd said, "Tell your father he's next." She couldn't get anybody to tell her what it meant. It was disturbing, like a comment she'd overheard that the man who'd put a knife in her, trying to kill her father, had been poisoned and died. Something big was going on, linked to that Wyoming murder, and to some politician who had ties to a drug cartel. But nobody told Carlie anything.

"Well, I'll be off. I have a meeting in San Antonio," Reverend Blair said, taking his leave. He paused at Carlie's desk. "Don't do anything fancy for supper, okay?" he asked, smiling. "I may be very late."

"Okay, Dad." She smiled at him.

He ruffled her hair, and walked out.

Carson was watching the interplay with cynical eyes.

"Doesn't your dad ruffle your hair?" she asked sarcastically.

"No. He did lay a chair across it once." He averted his eyes at once, as if the comment had slipped out and embarrassed him.

Carlie tried not to stare. What in the world sort of background did he come from? The violence struck a chord in her. She had secrets of her own from years past.

"Carson," Garon Grier said, pausing at the door. "We may need you at some point."

Carson nodded. "I'll be around."

"Thanks."

Garon waved at Grier, smiled at Carlie and let himself out the door.

"Something perking?" Carson asked Grier.

"Quite a lot, in fact. Carlie, hold my calls until I tell you," he instructed.

"Sure thing, Boss."

"Come on in." Cash went ahead, into his office.

Carson paused by Carlie's desk and glared at her.

She glared back. "If you don't stop scowling at me, I'm going to ask the chief to frisk you for hand grenades," she muttered.

"Frisk me yourself," he dared softly.

The flush deepened, darkened.

His black eyes narrowed, because he knew innocence when he saw it. It was rare in his world. "Clueless, aren't you?" he chided.

She lifted her chin and glared back. "My father is a minister," she said with quiet pride.

"Really?"

She frowned, cocking her head. "Excuse me?"

"Are you coming in, or not?" Cash asked suddenly, and there was a bite in his voice.

Carson seemed faintly surprised. He followed

Cash into the office. The door closed. There was a remark spoken in a harsh tone, followed by a pause and a suddenly apologetic one.

Carlie paid little attention. Carson had upset her nerves. She wished her boss would find someone else to talk to. Her job had been wonderful and satisfying until Carson started hanging around all the time. Something was going on, something big. It involved local and federal law enforcement—she was fairly certain that the chief's brother didn't just happen by to visit—and somehow it also involved her father.

She wondered if she could dig any information out of her parent if she went about it in the right way. She'd have to work on that.

She wondered if all the traffic through her boss's office involved her in some way, as well as her father. The attack, the death of the assailant and the strange call were frightening. She still wondered why anybody would attack a minister.

That remark of Carson's made her curious. She'd said her father was a minister and he'd said, "Really?" in that sarcastic, cold tone of voice. When he'd gone into Cash's office, there had been hard words. Had Carson said something Cash didn't want her to hear? And why?

"I'm a mushroom," she said to herself. "They

keep me in the dark and feed me manure." She sighed and went back to work.

SHE WAS ON the phone with the sheriff's office when Carson left. He went by her desk with only a cursory glance at her, and it was, of all things, placid. Almost apologetic. She lowered her eyes and refused to even look at him.

Even if she'd found him irresistible—and she was trying not to—his reputation with women put her off. Carlie was a small-town girl, raised religiously, and she didn't share the casual attitude of many of her former classmates.

She grimaced. In school, they'd made fun of her, and whispered about her. One pretty, popular girl had said that she didn't know what she was missing and that she should lose those outdated morals and live it up.

Carlie had just stared and her and smiled. She didn't say anything. Apparently the smile wore the other girl down because she shrugged, turned her back and walked off to whisper to the girls in her circle. They all looked at Carlie and laughed.

She was used to it. Her father said that adversity was like grit—it honed metal to a fine edge. She'd have liked to be honed a little less.

They were right about one thing: she really didn't know what she was missing. She'd read books that told about those sensations she was supposed to feel with men and she didn't feel any of them.

She chided herself silently. That was a lie. She felt them when she was close to Carson. She knew that he was aware of it, which made it worse. He laughed at her, just the way her classmates had laughed at her in school. She was the odd one out, the misfit. She had a reason for her ironclad morals. Many local people knew them, too. Episodes in her childhood had hardened her.

Well, people tended to be products of their upbringing. That was life. Unless she wanted to throw away her ideals and give up religion, she was pretty much settled in her beliefs. Maybe it wasn't so bad being a misfit. Her late grandfather had said that civilizations rested on the bedrock of faith and law and the arts. Some people had to be conventional to keep the mechanism going.

"What was that?" Sheriff Hayes's receptionist asked.

"Sorry." Carlie cleared her throat. She'd been on hold. "I was just mumbling to myself. What were you saying?"

The woman laughed and gave her the information the chief had asked for, about an upcoming criminal case.

SHE COOKED A light supper, just creamed chicken and rice, with green peas, and made a nice apple pie for dessert.

Her father came in, looking harassed. Then he saw the spread and grinned from ear to ear. "What a nice surprise!"

"I know, something light. But I was hungry," she added.

He made a face. "Shame. Telling lies."

She shrugged. "I went to church Sunday. God won't mind a little lie, in a good cause."

He smiled. "You know, some people have actually asked me how to talk to God."

"I just do it while I'm cooking, or working in the yard," Carlie said. "Just like I'm talking to you."

He laughed. "Me, too. But there are people who make hard work of it."

"Why were you in the chief's office today?" she asked.

He paused in the act of putting a napkin in his lap. His expression went blank for an instant, then it came back to life. "He wanted me to talk to a prisoner for him," he said finally.

She raised both eyebrows.

"Sorry," he said, smoothing out the napkin. "Some things are confidential."

"Okay."

"Let's say grace," he added.

LATER, HE watched the news while she cleaned up the kitchen. She sat down with him and turned off the news so they could watch a nature special. Then she excused herself and went upstairs to read. She wasn't really interested in much television programming, except for history specials and anything about mining. She loved rocks.

She sat down on the side of her bed and thumbed through her bookshelf. Most titles were digital as well as physical these days, but she still loved the feel and smell of an actual book in her hands.

She pulled out a well-worn copy of a book on the Little Bighorn fight, one that was written by members of various tribes who'd actually been present. It irritated her that many of the soldiers had said there were no living witnesses to the battle. That was not true. There were plenty of them: Lakota, Cheyenne, Crow and a host of other men from different tribes who were at the battle and saw exactly what happened.

She smiled as she read about how many of them ended up in Buffalo Bill Cody's famous traveling Wild West Show. They played before the crowned heads of Europe. They learned high society manners and how to drink tea from a fancy china cup. They laughed among themselves at the irony of it. Sitting Bull himself worked for Cody for a time, before he was killed.

She loved most to read about Crazy Horse. Like Carson, he was Lakota Sioux. He was light-skinned and a great tactician. There was only one verified photograph of him, which was disputed by some, accepted by others. It showed a rather handsome man with pigtails, wearing a breastplate. There was also a sketch. He had led a war party against General Crook at the Battle of Washita and won it. He led another party against Custer at the Little Bighorn.

Until his death, by treachery at the hands of a soldier, he was the most famous war leader of the Lakota. Sitting Bull did not fight; he was not a warrior. He was a holy man who made medicine and had visions of a great battle that was won by the Native tribes.

Crazy Horse fascinated Carlie. She bought book after book looking for all she could find in his history.

She knew about battles, because her secret vice was an online video game, "World of Warcraft." A number of people in Jacobsville and Comanche Wells played. She knew the gamer tags, the names in-game, of only a very few. Probably she'd partnered with some of them in raid groups. But mostly she ran battlegrounds, in player versus player matches, but only on weekends, when she had more free time.

Gaming took the place of dates she never got. She could be attractive when she tried, but she wasn't really pretty and she was painfully shy around people she didn't know. She'd only gone out a couple of times in high school, once with a boy who was getting even with his girlfriend by dating her—although Carlie hadn't known until later—and another with a boy who saw her as an easy mark and got a big surprise.

From time to time she thought about how nice it would be to marry and have children. She loved spending time in the baby section of department stores when she went to San Antonio with her father occasionally. She liked to look at knitted booties and lacy little dresses.

She settled in with her new copy of a book on Alexander the Great. The phone rang. She got up, but she didn't want to answer it. She recalled the threat from the unknown man and wondered if that was him.

She went to the staircase and hesitated. Her father was on the phone.

"Yes, I know," he said in a tone he'd never used with her. "If you think you can do better, you're welcome to try." He paused and a huge sigh left his chest. "Listen, she's all I've got in the world. I know I don't deserve her, but I will never let anyone harm her. This place may not look secure, but I assure you, it is…"

He leaned against the wall near the phone table, with the phone in his hand. He looked world-weary. "That's what I thought, too, at first," he said quietly. "I still have enemies. But it isn't me he's after. It's Carlie! It has to have something to do with the man she saw in Grier's office. I know that the man who killed Joey and masqueraded as a DEA agent is dead. But if he put out a contract before he died…Yes, that's what I'm telling you." He shook his head. "I know you don't have the funds. It's okay. I have plenty of people who owe me favors. I'll call in a few. Yes. I do appreciate your help. It's just…it's worrying me, that's all. Sure. I'll call you. Thanks." He hung up.

Carlie moved back into the shadows. Her father looked like a stranger, someone she'd never seen before. She wondered who he'd been speaking to, and if the conversation was about her. It sounded that way. What was a contract? A contract to kill someone? She bit her lower lip. Something to do with the man she saw in the chief's office, the man she'd tried to describe for the artist, the DEA agent who wasn't an agent.

She frowned. But he was dead. Her father had said he was dead. Then he'd mentioned that con-tract, that the man might have put it out before he died. From what she'd been able to learn, the dead man was the one she'd seen. If he was dead, why did it matter that she'd seen him? Of course, if he'd wanted her dead so she couldn't tell people about him, and some unknown person had been paid in advance to kill her...

She swallowed down the fear. She could be killed by mistake, by a dead man's contract killer. How ironic. Her father had said the house was safe. She wondered why he said that, what he knew. For the first time in her life, she wondered who her father really was....

SHE FIXED HIM a nice breakfast. While they were eating it she averted her eyes and said, "Why do you think that man came to kill me?"

His coffee cup paused halfway to his mouth. "What?"

"The man with the knife."

"We agreed that he was after me, didn't we?" he said.

She lifted her eyes and stared at him. "I work for the police. It's impossible not to learn a little something about law enforcement in the process. That man wasn't after you at all, was he? The man they poisoned, so he couldn't tell what he knew?"

He let out a breath and put the coffee cup down. "Well, Carlie, you're more perceptive than I gave you credit for." He smiled faintly. "Must be my genes. Your mother, God rest her soul, didn't have that gift. She saw everything in black-and-white."

"Yes, she did." Talk of her mother made her sad. It had just been Carlie and Mary for a long time, until Mary got sick. After she passed away, Carlie's father came back from a mission and got her. They'd been together ever since.

"We're still not sure he didn't come after me," her father said, interrupting her reveries.

"I heard you talking on the phone last night," she said.

He grimaced. "Bad timing on my part." He sighed.

"Very bad. So now I know. Tell me what's going on."

"That phone call you had came from a San Antonio number. We traced it, but it led to a throw-away phone," he replied. "That's bad news."

"Why?"

"Because sometimes those phones are used by criminals to escape detection by the authorities. They use the phone once to connect with people who might be wiretapped, then they dispose of the phone. Drug lords buy them by the cartload," he added.

"Well, I didn't do anybody in over a drug deal, and the guy I gave the artist the description of died in Wyoming. So why is somebody still after me?" she concluded.

He smiled. "Smart. Very smart. The guy died. That's the bottom line. If he hired somebody to go after you, to keep you from recognizing him in a future lineup, it's too late to call him off. Get the picture?"

"In living color," she said. She felt very adult, having her father give her the truth instead of a sweet lie to calm her.

"I have a couple of friends watching you," he said. "I don't think it's a big threat, but we'd be insane not to take it seriously, especially after what's already happened."

"That was almost three months ago," she began.

"Yes, at the beginning of a long chain of growing evidence." He sipped coffee. "I still can't believe how many people's lives have been impacted by this man and whoever he was working for."

"You have some idea who his boss is…was?"

He nodded. "I can't tell you, so don't ask. I will say that several law enforcement agencies are involved."

"I still don't understand why you're having meetings with my boss and that…that man Carson."

He studied her flushed face. "I've heard about

Carson's attitude toward you. If he keeps it up, I'll have a talk with him."

"Don't," she asked softly. "With any luck, he won't be around long. He doesn't strike me as a man who likes small towns or staying in one place for any length of time."

"You never know. He likes working for Cy Parks. And he has a few projects going with locals."

She groaned.

"I can talk to him nicely."

"Sure, Dad, and then he'll accuse me of running to Daddy for protection." She lifted her chin. "I can take whatever he can hand out."

He smiled at her stubbornness. "Okay."

She made a face. "He just doesn't like me, that's all. Maybe I remind him of someone he doesn't care for."

"That's possible." He stared into his coffee cup. "Or it could have something to do with asking him for a grenade to start a fire...."

"Aww, now, I wasn't trying to do anything," she protested.

He chuckled. "Sure." He studied her face. "I just want to mention one thing," he added gently. "He's not housebroken. And he never will be. Just so you know."

"I have never wanted to housebreak a wolf, I assure you."

"There's also his attitude about women. He makes no secret of it." His face hardened. "He likens them to party favors. Disposable. You understand?"

"I understand. But honestly, that's not the sort of man I'd be seriously interested in. You don't have to worry."

"I do worry. You're not street-smart, pumpkin," he added, with the pet name that he almost never used. "You're unworldly. A man like that could be dangerous to you…."

She held up a hand. "I have weapons."

He blinked. "Excuse me?"

"If he starts showing any interest in me, I'll give him my most simpering smile and start talking about how I'd love to move in with him that very day and start having children at once." She wiggled her eyebrows. "Works like a charm. They actually leave skid marks…."

"Exactly." He looked at his watch. "Well, I have a meeting with the church officials. We're working on an outreach program for the poor. Something I really want to do."

She smiled. "You know, you really are the nicest minister I know."

He bent and kissed her forehead before he left.

"Thanks, sweetheart. Be sure to check your truck, okay?"

She laughed. "I always do. Don't worry."

He hesitated. He wanted to tell her that he did worry, and the whole reason why. But it was the wrong time.

She was already halfway in love with Carson. He knew things about the man that he'd been told in confidence. He couldn't repeat them. But if Curlie got too close to that prowling wolf, he'd leave scars that would cripple her for life. It was like seeing a wire break and being too far away to fix it before it started a fire.

He could talk to Carson, of course. But that would only make matters worse. He had to wait and hope that Carlie could ignore the man's practiced charms if he ever used them on her. And Carson would. It was just a matter of time. He could tell....

New York Times bestselling author

SUSAN MALLERY

invites readers back to her beloved series set in Fool's Gold featuring three newcomers who find love when they are least expecting it...

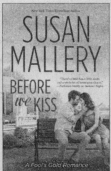

Available now wherever books are sold!

"Susan Mallery is one of my favorites."
—#1 _New York Times_ bestselling author Debbie Macomber

HARLEQUIN® HQN™
www.Harlequin.com

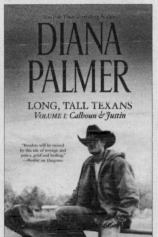

DIANA PALMER

77854	PROTECTOR	___ $7.99 U.S.	___ $8.99 CAN.
77762	COURAGEOUS	___ $7.99 U.S.	___ $9.99 CAN.
77727	NOELLE	___ $7.99 U.S.	___ $9.99 CAN.
77724	WYOMING BOLD	___ $7.99 U.S.	___ $8.99 CAN.
77696	WYOMING FIERCE	___ $7.99 U.S.	___ $9.99 CAN.
77666	MERCILESS	___ $7.99 U.S.	___ $9.99 CAN.
77633	LACY	___ $7.99 U.S.	___ $9.99 CAN.
77631	NORA	___ $7.99 U.S.	___ $9.99 CAN.
77570	DANGEROUS	___ $7.99 U.S.	___ $9.99 CAN.
77283	LAWMAN	___ $7.99 U.S.	___ $7.99 CAN.

(limited quantities available)

TOTAL AMOUNT	$_____
POSTAGE & HANDLING	$_____
($1.00 FOR 1 BOOK, 50¢ for each additional)	
APPLICABLE TAXES*	$_____
TOTAL PAYABLE	$_____

(check or money order—please do not send cash)

To order, complete this form and send it, along with a check or money order for the total above, payable to Harlequin HQN, to: **In the U.S.:** 3010 Walden Avenue, P.O. Box 9077, Buffalo, NY 14269-9077; **In Canada:** P.O. Box 636, Fort Erie, Ontario, L2A 5X3.

Name: _____

Address: _____ City: _____

State/Prov.: _____ Zip/Postal Code: _____

Account Number (if applicable): _____

075 CSAS

*New York residents remit applicable sales taxes.
*Canadian residents remit applicable GST and provincial taxes.

HARLEQUIN® HQN™
www.Harlequin.com

PHDP0714BL